PUFFIN BOOKS

Editor: Kaye Webb

More Tales of Shellover

There never was such a creature for storytelling as
Shellover. Perhaps it was all that deep winter-dream-
ing he did when he lay buried under his cold earth-
blanket that filled his mind with such a variety of
strange, magical tales, or perhaps it was just that he
travelled so slowly that he had time to think things
up. Anyway, whatever it was, it was a great treat for
Mrs Candy and all her other animal friends when
Shellover woke up in spring and started his spellbind-
ing stories again.

They loved the story about Speckle, the strange
little feathered fairy girl who hatched out of an egg,
and of Mrs Crabapple the lonely witch who scared
the neighbours into fits when she innocently asked
them in to a housewarming party, and about the sea
baby who was caught in the fisherman's net, and the
strange tale of Tim and Billy and the talking snow-
men ...

Yes, Shellover the storytelling tortoise was a
splendid creature to have around. In fact, the only
trouble with him was that he *would* get sleepy when
the autumn came.

Ruth Ainsworth's earlier book, *The Ten Tales of
Shellover*, is already a firm favourite in Young Puffins,
like her collections of poems and stories, *Lucky Dip*
and *Another Lucky Dip*.

For readers of six and over.

RUTH AINSWORTH

MORE TALES OF SHELLOVER

Illustrated by Antony Maitland

PUFFIN BOOKS

Puffin Books Penguin Books Ltd, Harmondsworth, Middlesex, England
Penguin Books, 625 Madison Avenue, New York, New York 10022, U.S.A.
Penguin Books Australia Ltd, Ringwood, Victoria, Australia
Penguin Books Canada Ltd, 41 Steelcase Road West, Markham, Ontario, Canada
Penguin Books (N.Z.) Ltd, 182–190 Wairau Road, Auckland 10, New Zealand

—

First published by André Deutsch Ltd 1968
Published in Puffin Books 1976

—

—

Made and printed in Great Britain by
Richard Clay (The Chaucer Press), Ltd,
Bungay, Suffolk
Set in Linotype Pilgrim

Contents

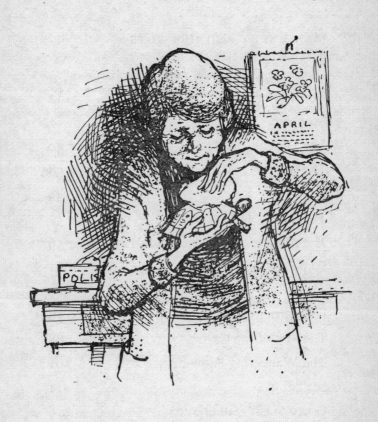

Mrs Candy and Her Pets

MRS CANDY was a kind old woman who lived in a cottage, and kept a great many pets. She loved them all as though they were her own dear children, and they loved her as if she were their own dear mother.

There was the Cat, who was so spoilt that he had to have a drop of hot water in his milk, to warm it.

There was the Dog, who carried sticks in his mouth and dropped them on the hearth to help Mrs Candy to light the fire.

There were the seven black Hens, who laid the most beautiful eggs, full of goodness.

Then there was the Cow, who gave rich, creamy milk for Mrs Candy and her family.

Last of all there was the new pet, Shellover the Tortoise, who spent the winter half of the year buried under the laurel bush, asleep. During the summer half of the year he was wide awake, creeping over the garden, and feasting on lettuces and other nourishing plants. He was always willing to tell stories if he were asked politely.

Sometimes Mrs Candy and her pets gathered under the apple tree for a story. Perhaps Mrs Candy had a bowl of gooseberries in her lap, to top and tail while she listened. But the stories were so interesting that she often forgot the gooseberries completely, and the scissors dropped out of her hand.

At other times, if Mrs Candy had had a busy day, she sat indoors in her rocking-chair, and the pets gathered round her, all except the Cow who was too big to come into the cottage. She stood outside in the garden, flicking the midges away with her tail, and poking her head through the window which Mrs Candy always left open for her.

Shellover the Tortoise, when he was indoors, sat on a special low, round footstool, which had pansies embroidered on it in wool. It had been worked by Mrs Candy's grandmother.

Shellover was very fond of pansies, especially yellow ones, and he liked sitting on the pansy stool. Mrs Candy lifted him on to it to tell the story, and lifted him off at the end.

The only trouble with Shellover was that when the cold days came, he just got sleepier and sleepier until at last he could keep awake no longer. Then he dug himself a hole in the garden for his winter sleep. The Dog helped to cover over the last square of his shell.

The animals felt dull and lonely without him, and were very glad when the winter was over at last and spring was com-ing. 'Surely,' they said, 'it is time for Shellover to wake up and tell us some more stories.'

'I'll soon dig him up,' said the Dog.

'I'll help to loosen the soil,' said the Cat.

'I'll walk round and round stamping my hoofs,' said the Cow. 'We'll see if *that* will waken him.'

'We'll scratch a little,' said the Hens. 'Just enough to let some air and sunshine into his dark hole.'

'He'll wake when he's ready,' said Mrs Candy. 'It won't be long now.'

The pets were not quite sure exactly where Shellover was sleeping. They had known once. They'd even watched him dig his hole. But so many things had happened since then; Christmas, and a fall of snow, and long, cold days that seemed all alike.

'I shall do a little digging under the currant bushes,' said the Dog.

'I shall try beside the lavender,' said the Cat.

'I seem to remember he was near the apple tree,' said the Cow.

'We think he's down here, by the hedge,' said the Hens.

In the end it was Mrs Candy who called out:

'Come quickly! Come quickly! Here he is!'

The pets gathered round a patch of soil under the laurel bush.

'Of course,' they said. 'Of course it was under the laurel bush. We remember now. It all comes back to us.'

The earth was cracking. It was crumbling. It was stirring. A little bit of Shellover's back appeared. Slowly and surely he was freeing himself from the soil. Soon he was all uncovered.

He put out his four stumpy legs, and his tail, and his neat, flat head. The Dog licked the remaining crumbs of soil off his shell, and everyone gave a sigh of joy. Shellover had come back to them. His long winter sleep was over.

Later in the day, Mrs Candy polished his shell with a spot of furniture cream, and he looked spick and span. That very same evening, the pets begged for a story, and Mrs Candy said it would have to be told indoors, as the evenings were chilly. So she sat in her rocking-chair, with the Cat on her lap, and the Dog at her feet, and the seven Hens perched along the back of the sofa. The Cow stood in the garden, and stretched her neck through the window. Mrs Candy could feel her soft breath, sweet as clover.

She lifted Shellover on to the pansy footstool, and he blinked a few times, and then began.

'My first story is about three friends. Once upon a time . . .'

Three Friends

MOONLIGHT was an old white horse who spent his days alone in a field. Once he had been young and frisky. Once he had pulled a farm cart laden with sacks of potatoes and sugar beet. But now be was too old to work. He nibbled the grass and dreamed in the sunshine. When the rain fell, he took shelter in a shed in the corner of the field.

Every day he had one treat. He spent half the day looking forward to it, and the other half looking back at it. At some time, he never knew exactly when it would be, the farmer who owned him brought him a bundle of oats or hay.

Moonlight did all he could to make the farmer stay and talk to him for a little while. He whinnied and tossed his head, and sometimes even nipped hold of the farmer's sleeve. But he was too gentle and well-mannered to grip it tightly. When the farmer turned to go with a brisk: 'See you tomorrow, old chap,' he loosened his hold at once.

Moonlight often thought that the farmer was busier than he used to be, even though he now possessed a tractor and a van and a car. In the old days, Moonlight could remember him resting in the shade of a tree and smoking his pipe; or leaning on the bridge while Moonlight drank from the flowing stream. Now he seemed almost too busy to breathe. It was all very strange and very sad.

One day, Moonlight was standing in the shelter of the hedge, as the wind was keen, thinking of old times. He remembered when he had been led to the Show, his mane and tail plaited, and his coat gleaming. He had won a rosette, and his master had been very proud of him. Suddenly he felt he was being watched. He looked down, and there, on the grass, was a small black hen with a red comb.

'Good morning, Moonlight,' said the hen.

'How did you know my name?' asked Moonlight.

'Oh those chattering sparrows know everything,' said the hen. 'Always gossiping, just listen to them!'

Sure enough, there was a commotion going on in the hedge where the sparrows were chirping and arguing.

'I don't pay much heed to feathered folk,' said Moonlight, 'or not since I left the farm. The farmyard birds had their uses, it can't be denied. There were geese with long necks, and ducks on the duck pond, and of course your relations were all over the yard. They were mostly speckled, I remember. Good layers, too. The farmer's wife collected a pailful of eggs every day about tea-time.'

'My laying days are over,' said the black hen sadly. 'Beautiful white eggs I laid, smooth and perfect, with yolks of pure gold.'

'Have you come far?' asked Moonlight.

'A fair way, a fair way,' said the hen. 'I won't go into details because those sparrows have sharp ears. The news might get around. Come nearer and I'll whisper something.'

Moonlight came nearer, being careful where he put his great hoofs, till his whiskery nose was almost touching the little black hen.

'I've run away,' she clucked softly. 'My life was in danger. I didn't lay any more eggs and they said I wasn't worth my keep. They planned to make me into chicken soup. I wasn't plump or tender enough to roast.'

'That was a shame!' said Moonlight. 'I've been lucky, I

know. I'm too old to work, but my master keeps me on for old time's sake. If he'd been a harder man, he'd have sold me for what I'd fetch. I'm lucky and I know it.'

'What do you do all day?' asked the hen.

'I walk about. I stand still. I think. And there's always the feeling that my dinner might be coming any minute. Look! There's my master coming now, I believe it's oats today.'

The little black hen scuttled into the hedge and stayed there while the farmer gave Moonlight his bundle of oats.

'See you tomorrow, old chap,' he said, as he strode away.

'You can come out now,' said Moonlight. 'You needn't have hidden in the first place. Come out and share my dinner.'

The hen came from under the hedge as Moonlight began eating and she pecked daintily at the oats. Her quick movements delighted Moonlight who had become stiff and slow with age.

'I've never enjoyed a meal more,' he said, as he lifted his head.

'Nor have I,' replied the hen. 'In the farmyard there was always such a struggle for the food, such pushing and jostling. Here it is so peaceful.'

'I'm alone too much,' went on Moonlight. 'I've almost forgotten how to talk, and I'd quite forgotten that food is better shared. Why, I've never even asked you your name.'

The hen hung her head, ashamed to confess that she hadn't got a name. But Moonlight understood.

'Then I shall call you Jet. Do you like it?'

'Yes,' said Jet, saying it softly over to herself. 'Yes, I do.'

Moonlight and Jet became close friends as the days went

by. Wherever Jet went, pecking at seeds and insects, Moonlight followed, careful where he placed his great hoofs.

When Moonlight lay down, Jet settled near him, until one wintry night there was a touch of frost. Moonlight retired to his shed and Jet followed.

'Are your feet cold, Jet?'

'They're chilly,' said Jet, 'but I don't mind. I've a roof over my head.'

'Then perch on me,' said Moonlight. 'I'm always warm.'

Jet flew up and perched on his back, her feet buried in his thick, white coat. After this she often sat on his back, after he had assured her that she weighed nothing at all.

'Just a puff of feathers, that's what you are,' he said.

Moonlight and Jet were different in every way, in size and shape and colour, and in their past experiences. When Moonlight told stories of the Show and the rosette he had won, Jet was entranced. When Jet told of how she had defended her eggs against a robber rat, Moonlight felt proud of her courage.

'I'd have sent that rat packing!' he said, stamping his hoof. 'He wouldn't have dared to show his ratty face again if I'd been around.'

One evening, they stayed awake late, Moonlight describing his childhood when he was a long-legged foal and had lived in a buttercup meadow with his mother. Jet then told of her early memories, when she was a ball of fluff among a dozen other fluffy balls, and of her careful mother calling 'Cluck! Cluck! Cluck!' She told of her father the cock, of whom she had been very frightened.

'He was so fine,' she said, 'in red and green and black, with such a majestic voice. I never dared lift my head to look at him properly. I just trembled.'

Moonlight referred to the time before Jet joined him as 'the bad old days', and Jet, when she spoke of her farmyard life, began the sentence with 'long, long, long ago'.

Then they made another friend. A little girl with long, dark plaits passed the gate of their field on her way to school, and she often called out: 'Hullo Moonlight! Hullo Jetty!' and Moonlight gave a friendly whinny, and Jet a polite cluck-cluck.

When they knew each other better, the little girl climbed on the gate and called: 'Coop! Coop! Coop!' Then Moonlight and Jet hurried to the gate and she took her dinner tin out of her satchel, opened it, brought out a biscuit and gave it to Moonlight. He took it gently with his soft lips before he crunched it up.

Then she broke off a corner of her cheese sandwich and crumbled it on the ground for Jet, who sought out every crumb.

This was another point of interest in each day, and always came at the same time, early in the morning.

Moonlight relished his biscuit.

'*Petit beurre* this morning,' he remarked to Jet, or, 'chocolate wholemeal for a change.'

Jet, too, enjoyed the crumbs of brown bread and cheese. Sometimes it was ham or sardines.

They liked the food, of course, but they also liked the little girl's fresh, clear voice, and the way her plaits swung when she leaned over the gate. Her name was Martha.

One day, Martha stopped on her way home from school at tea-time, and climbed on the gate.

'Coop! Coop! Coop!' she called, and Moonlight and Jet hurried towards her, though they knew her dinner tin was empty.

'I've something to think about, and you can help me,' said Martha, patting Moonlight's soft cheeks, and stroking Jet who spread her wings to show how she liked it.

'We are going to start a Nature Table at school, a special table under the window where we can put anything nice that we find, flowers or twigs or toadstools or anything alive. You live in the field and have all the time in the world to explore it. Perhaps you can show me if you find anything interesting?'

The two friends nodded their heads and looked serious. When Martha had run off, her plaits flapping, they began to look around. It was spring, and their field was full of new and exciting sights.

'I shall show her the chaffinch's nest,' said Jet.

'She can't take that away,' said Moonlight.

'Of course not, but she might like to see it. It's so very pretty, so green and mossy.'

'I shall show her the white violets and the first cowslip,' said Moonlight.

When Martha passed the gate in the morning she gave Moonlight his biscuit (it was a pat-a-cake that day), and she crumbled some cheese sandwich for Jet. Then, when they had finished their snack, she said:

'I'm five minutes early today, so I have time to look at anything you've found.'

Moonlight led her straight to the bank where the white violets grew, and Martha picked three violets and three leaves. Then he showed her the first cowslip.

'I'll pick it,' said Martha, 'because there are so many others in bud. They'll be out tomorrow.' She took a bud, too, and a leaf.

Jet was fluttering her wings and clucking, and it was obvious that she had something to show, too.

'Only to peep at,' she whispered, 'not to touch.'

Martha followed her very quietly and took one look at the chaffinch's nest, a soft, deep, mossy cup, and a quick look at a hedge-sparrow's nest, with eggs in it as blue as the sky.

'Thank you, thank you,' she said, when they were once more near the gate. 'I shan't tell anyone where they are. It will be a secret for you and me and Moonlight. I shall write about them in the Nature Calendar that hangs above the Nature Table. I'll try to draw them as well, but of course no blue could be blue enough for the eggs.'

Martha stopped and unstrapped her satchel again and took out her crayons and her pencil sharpener. She sharpened the blue one for the eggs, and the green one for moss, and the brown one for the dried grass. Then she heard the school bell, and quickly bundled everything back, and ran off, calling:

'See you this afternoon.'

As the days went by, Martha got to know every inch of the field, guided by Moonlight and Jet. She explored the pond in the far corner where frog spawn floated, and pussy willows grew. She learned to step carefully to avoid the mother lark on her nest in a tuft of grass, invisible unless you knew exactly where to look.

Later on the midges were very troublesome in the evenings, teasing and tickling. Moonlight shook his head and ears, twitched his whiskers, and stamped with his hoofs. But if the cloud moved off for a moment, it soon formed again. Jet spent hours fanning the midges away with her wings, glad to do something for her friend.

Martha got to know about the midges and their torments. She came one Saturday morning carrying an old, shady, straw hat. She had poked two holes in the crown for Moonlight's two ears to go through. It had once been a very pretty hat belonging to her grandmother, and it still had a wreath of forget-me-nots and daisies round it. There were three red cherries dangling at the back. They looked so real that

Jet pecked one gently, to convince herself they were not edible.

Moonlight was delighted with his new hat. It gave him shade from the sun for his dim old eyes, and some protection from the midges, all in one.

Martha's father came along with his camera and took a picture of Moonlight in his straw hat, which he wore slightly on one side. Jet perched on his back and held her head high, and Martha stood beside him, her hand on his neck. When the village held its Photographic Exhibition in the autumn, the photo won a prize.

It was called: THREE FRIENDS.

Speckle

ONCE upon a time, a man and his wife lived in a forest with their five children. Four of the children were boys, tough, strong, sun-burned lads, always wearing holes in the elbows of their jackets and the soles of their boots. The fifth child was a girl named Cathy, gentler and more timid than her big brothers.

Cathy was often alone, playing by herself, because she was not old enough to race about with her brothers. One day, she took the big bag off the nail on the back door, and went out to gather sticks. She liked gathering sticks and was careful to pick up only dry ones that would burn well, leaving the ones that were damp or green or rotten.

There had been a high wind the night before and the ground was littered with sticks. Cathy soon filled her bag. Then she noticed a bent old woman, also picking up sticks. But the old woman was not darting here and there like Cathy, she was hobbling slowly along, groaning as she stooped down. She carried a rush basket, but it was nowhere near full. She was getting on so slowly that it would be sunset before she had gathered a good store.

'Let me help you,' said Cathy shyly, propping her own stuffed bag against a tree-trunk. 'Here's a handful of ash – my mother likes ash sticks best. And a handful of oak – they are good, too. And here are a few fir cones. They are useful when you start the fire. Sit down in that patch of sun and rest, and I'll soon fill your basket.'

The old woman sat and rested, while Cathy skipped

about, gathering sticks like a fairy. When the basket would hold no more she brought it to the old woman.

'Thank you, my dear,' said the old woman. 'One good turn deserves another. Here is a speckled egg. Keep it warm and it will hatch and give you a surprise.'

'May I really have it for my own?' said Cathy. 'My mother has some black hens, but they never lay speckled eggs. I do hope it will hatch out. But,' she added, 'you needn't have given me anything. I would have gathered the sticks for nothing.'

The old woman hobbled off and Cathy walked carefully home with the egg tucked down the front of her dress for warmth.

'Mother,' she cried, as she opened the door, 'an old lady has given me a speckled egg. She says it will hatch out if I keep it warm.'

'Very well,' said her mother. 'Slip it under the old hen who is sitting on a clutch of eggs in the shed. She'll not mind having another one. She can't count.'

So Cathy slipped the speckled egg under the hen with the other eggs. When the right time came, the eggs began to crack and out came balls of yellow fluff, each calling, 'Cheep! Cheep! Cheep!' and nestling under its mother's sheltering wings. The speckled egg hatched last of all, and out came a little creature covered with speckled feathers, crying, 'Ee! Ee! Ee!'

'There's a queer chick in that batch,' said Cathy's mother. 'It's crying more like a baby than a chick.' She picked up the little speckled thing and at once turned pale, and her hand shook.

'Cathy – you take it.'

'How lovely!' said Cathy, taking the little creature. 'It

isn't a chicken at all. It's a little girl no bigger than my finger. She's all dressed in feathers, but she has hair like mine and a face like mine and proper hands and feet.'

'You'd better keep her for your own,' said her mother. 'The hen might peck her or tread on her and that would be the end of her.'

'Of course I'll take care of her,' said Cathy happily. 'I shall call her "Speckle" and love her as if she were my own sister.'

Cathy, now, had no time to feel lonely. Speckle kept her busy all day long. She washed her and combed her hair and gave her her food on the doll's tea-set. She put her to bed at night and got her up in the morning. She played with her and sang to her and comforted her if she fell over, or woke after a bad dream.

Speckle grew taller and fatter, but though she slept well and ate well, it was clear that she was going to stay a little thing, no bigger than a doll. She learned what a real child learns and could soon sing and dance, work and play, knit and sew, like Cathy herself.

But there was one thing that neither Cathy nor her father and mother, nor anyone else in the cottage, could teach Speckle. They could not teach her how to be good. She told lies as often as the truth. She pinched and bit and scratched if she was cross. Worst of all, she teased and tormented the other children till they were miserable and tried to hide from her. But she soon found them, running everywhere on her thin little legs and searching with her beady black eyes.

Once, when she had broken Cathy's best doll in a fit of temper, Cathy's mother shut her up in a box as a punishment, but she just curled up like a dormouse and went to sleep.

24

Another time, she cut the clothes' line and let the washing fall on to the dirty ground and Cathy's father gave her a slap. But she just laughed and ran in and out and round about, calling: 'You can't catch me! You can't catch me!'

As the weeks went by, and Speckle behaved worse instead of better, even the gentle, loving Cathy wished she had never seen the speckled egg, or troubled to hatch it out.

One day, Cathy's father was walking at the edge of the forest when he came upon a grassy hill. There were fairy rings of dark grass on it and he knew it was the home of some of the Little People. As he paused, he saw a group of Little People trying to roll a stone towards a hole in the hillside. They were pushing as hard as they could, but the stone was not moving an inch.

He took off his hat and bowed and asked if he could help. The Little People smiled and nodded, and he pushed the stone into the mouth of the hole with one hand. The Queen of the Little People appeared, dressed in white and followed by six ladies in green.

'You have saved my people many days' labour,' she said. 'We need that rock for a new grinding stone. I will grant you a wish before you return to your home. What shall it be?'

Cathy's father did not hesitate. 'Please, your majesty, will you tell me how to make our little Speckle a good child. We love her, bad though she is, but we wish she would love us in return.'

'There's only one way to change her,' said the Queen. 'She must shed tears for someone or something not herself. Then she will be as good and loving as your own Cathy.'

'How can I make her cry?' asked Cathy's father. 'She feels neither pain nor grief?' But the door into the hillside had closed. The Little People had vanished like morning dew. There were only the narrow grasses at his feet, bending as the wind went by.

When he told his wife and children about his meeting with the Fairy Queen, they listened carefully, but shook their heads when they heard what the Queen had said.

'She never feels sorry for anyone,' said his wife.

'She *likes* people to be unhappy,' said the four boys.

'When I cry, she laughs and dances,' said Cathy.

'Whatever shall we do?'

The mother found a book of stories and read the sad ones to the children in the evenings. Her own children wiped their eyes and blew their noses when the sad parts came, but Speckle just smiled to herself.

The father sang a sad song about two little children lost in a wood, who lay down to sleep and the robins covered them with strawberry leaves. His own children looked sorrowful, but Speckle threaded berries on a string and hummed to herself.

'We will fetch the Fiddler of the Dale,' said the mother. 'They say his tunes are so sweet and so sad that even the stones on the hillside weep, and the flowers of the field hang their heads.'

So the Fiddler of the Dale was brought. He was an old man, with flowing white hair and a long cloak. When he lifted his bow and played, the fire stopped crackling and the cat and the dog listened, the cat staring with her green eyes and the dog with his brown ones. Below the open window, the hens and their chicks gathered to hear, never stirring a foot or a feather.

The music was so beautiful that the listeners felt the tears rolling down their cheeks; all except Speckle, who was playing with an acorn cup and did not seem to hear.

'It's no good,' sighed the father and mother, after the Fiddler of the Dale had gone. 'Our little Speckle will never cry for anyone else's sorrows. We must bear with her tiresome ways and love her just the same.'

When Christmas drew near and the first snow fell, Speckle came running in with something nearly as big as herself in her arms.

'Look, mother,' she said. 'I've found a bird and it's so cold that it can't fly. I'll warm it by the fire.'

She knelt on the rug and laid the bird gently down.

'Let me look,' said the father, stamping the snow off his boots. 'Why, you needn't waste your time. The bird is dead. See, its eyes are closed and its claws are curled up. It's stiff and cold. I'll bury it for you.'

'Dead?' repeated Speckle. 'Dead? But I don't want it to

be dead and cold. I want it to be alive and warm, and to fly again.'

'Don't fret, little lass,' said the father. 'That little bird will never fly again.'

'Never fly again,' repeated Speckle. 'Are you sure?'

'Yes, I'm sure. But don't take on so. Somewhere in the world an egg-shell is cracking and a baby bird is hatching out to take the place of this one.'

'Never fly again,' cried Speckle, bursting into tears and sobbing. 'Poor little thing! Poor, poor little thing!'

When she could cry no more, she sat on the mother's lap and was kissed and comforted. From that moment, she was a different little person. She was gay and lively, but never played unkind tricks or was glad when other children were unhappy.

'Whatever should I do without my dear Speckle,' said Cathy, stroking the soft feathers. 'I shall never again have such a wonderful present as that little speckled egg.'

The Hole in the Tree

JAMES walked round and round the adventure playground by himself. Once he had a swing on one of the rubber tyres that hung there to swing on. Once he got on the last seat of the iron horse that some other children were riding. But mostly he just watched. So many of the things were best when there were two or three to play on them. He was only one. Still, there was the climbing frame and he climbed on that for a time.

There was a plain wall that the children could paint on, and afterwards the paintings could all be washed off, ready for the next lot. Someone was doing a long green train with many coaches. Someone else was doing what looked like a big sun with rays coming from it. Or was it a big sunflower? James would have liked to ask the little girl who was doing it, but he was far too shy.

James was shy, and he also felt strange. The old flat where he used to live had been pulled down. It wasn't a very nice flat, with small, dark rooms, but it had been his home since he was born. There was a tree at the corner of the street which he was fond of. In the autumn its leaves fell, and he used to pick some of them up and take them home. He liked walking through the fallen leaves, too, and hearing them rustle.

Now his family had moved to a shining, new block of flats, where lifts flashed up and down, and the balconies were painted red and black. James spent hours on his red and black balcony, looking out and watching other people doing things. Some of the things he would like to have done himself.

Although the new flats were only a little way from the old ones, it was like a different world. It also meant moving to a new school. The new school, like the new flats, was bright and shining, with gleaming paint and big windows. He liked it, but he wasn't used to it. He hadn't made any special friend yet.

A few days later James went to the adventure playground again. Directly he got there he knew something exciting had happened. Something was different. He could hear the children shouting and laughing before he got there. Soon he felt excited too. Since his last visit, a whole tree with branches had been put in a big, open space. It was not standing upright. It was not growing. It was lying on its side, just as it had been unloaded off a great big lorry.

James wondered where it had been when it was alive. Perhaps somewhere where the land was needed for houses or flats for people to live in. People couldn't live in a tree. But birds could, thought James, and insects.

The big boys and girls were climbing all over the tree, swinging on its branches and trying to get from one end to the other.

'I'm on a ship!' shouted one.

'I'm on a horse!' shouted another.

Some girls found a bird's nest and took it carefully to the warden.

'It's a very old one,' said the warden. 'It has only dead leaves in it. The birds will be building a new one some-where else.'

One of the little girls took the nest away, and said she

would make some clay eggs and put them in. Another girl said she would make a clay bird to sit on the eggs. They ran off to the shed where the clay was kept.

James thought what a good idea, and he thought of the little clay birds hatching out of the little clay eggs, and flying away. Of course that was nonsense, but he liked to think of them just the same.

James made up his mind to climb on the tree himself, but he wanted to be alone on the tree. He was only small, and the tree was very big. He was not sure if he *could* get on it. But he was going to try.

A few days later there was no one playing on the tree This was because the warden had got some big drain pipes, some long, some short, and some in between. They were so big that the children could crawl through them. Some were very long and only the bigger children dared to crawl in one end and out of the other. Everyone wanted a turn.

This was James's chance. He hurried to the tree and started climbing on the thin end, that had once been the top. It was hard because the branches stuck out in such awkward places. When he had got only a little way, it was time to go home.

The next time James had the tree to himself he got along the part he knew quite quickly, and then went further. He found that being small did not matter. He could squeeze between the branches and find places for his feet easily. He did very well. Sometimes he felt like a monkey that lived in the tree. He wished there were some coconuts for him to pick, or some bananas.

He was just pretending to be a monkey when his hand felt something odd. It was a little hole in the bark. But it did not look like a hole that belonged to the tree. It looked like a hole that someone had made bigger and deeper. It was not easy to see. He just felt it by chance with his finger. He looked again. Someone had dug at the hole with a pen-knife.

He put his finger in as far as it would go. He could feel some paper. He tried with his little finger, but he still could not get the paper out. Then he tried with his penknife. Even if it was an old bus ticket or a sweet paper he wanted to get it out. He prodded and prodded and out it came.

It was plain paper with some writing on it. He put it in his pocket, climbed off the tree, and ran home.

When he was on his balcony he undid the paper. The writing was in pencil, and the paper was creased all over from being folded up so tightly. The writing said:

Peter. 12A Back Row.
I have a million friends.

James was very pleased when he read the words. He did not take much notice of *a million friends* but he did take notice of the address, 12A *Back Row*. He had once lived at 11A Front Row, and Back Row was the next street. It was going to be pulled down soon, he had heard.

He made a plan in his head. The next day was Sunday and he asked his mother if he could go back to where they used to live, to see what it looked like.

'Go if you like,' she said, 'but I don't think many people we knew will be left there. Be careful, and don't be too long.'

James ran all the way. The road was being widened where he used to live. Then he went along Back Row. The houses up to No. 10 had gone. He stopped by No. 12A. He stopped and waited. While he waited and looked about, he noticed the tree had gone from the corner. There was only a stump left.

Soon a little boy with dark, untidy hair came out and began kicking a stone along the gutter. James went up to him and before he had time to feel shy, he said:

'Are you Peter?'

'Yes,' said the boy.

'Then is this yours?' He held out the paper.

'Why yes, it is. Where did you find it?'

'Where you left it.'

'In the hole in the tree?'

'Yes.'

'But where is the tree? It used to be at the end of Back Row, but they cut it down last week. I used to climb it.'

'You still can climb it,' said James. 'It's in our adventure playground, near where I live.'

'We're moving pretty soon to some new flats,' said Peter. 'All my friends have gone. I shan't know anyone in the new place.'

'Then why did you write that you had a million friends?'

Peter did not say anything for a long time. Then he said:

'I guess I wrote it because I hadn't any friends at all. They've gone. I guess I was just pretending.'

James thought about this. It was just how he felt. He hadn't any friends either.

'I'm like you,' he said to Peter. 'I haven't any friends. Would you like to come and see your tree?'

'I would,' said Peter. 'I would very much.'

They ran off together and soon they were both playing on Peter's tree. They played at being monkeys. Then they played at hiding from the enemy. Then it got dark, and both boys went home.

'See you after school tomorrow,' said James.

'Sure, I'll be there,' said Peter.

Peter soon moved to the same block of flats where James lived. He started at James's school and they played together at break, and after school in the adventure playground, and all the weekend.

They often looked at the hole in the tree where James had found Peter's message. One day James said:

'I've written something else to put in your hole.'

'Show me.'

James handed over a scrap of paper and Peter read:

I have one friend and his name is Peter.

Then they both laughed, and James rolled up the paper very, very small, and poked it into the hole.

That day they tried crawling down the drain pipes. It was fun, and they crawled down them all, even the very long, dark one.

But playing on Peter's tree, which was now James's tree as well, was better still. They liked it best of all.

The Dancers in Green

A LITTLE brother and sister lived in a stone castle. The castle had large, heavy gates which were guarded by two guards. All round there was a thick, high yew hedge. It was so high that the children could not look over it, and so thick that they could not see through it. The yew hedge was dark green, and once a year it bore little pink fruits. Their parents wanted them to play within the safety of this hedge until they were old enough to look after themselves.

There were many things the children could do in the garden. There were fountains where they could bathe, and lily ponds where they could float their boats. There was a swing and a see-saw, and many shady, secret places among the bushes where they could hide. But they were not content with all this. They wanted to see what was on the other side of the yew hedge.

Sometimes they walked all round the castle, keeping close to the hedge, and looking for a gap or a thin place that they could wriggle through. But the hedge was as thick and solid as a stone wall.

Once they tried to make a hole by breaking off the twigs, one by one. Their fingers grew sore, but the hedge stayed as thick as ever.

One day, the little girl came running to her brother.

'Come quickly!' she said. 'You'll never guess what I have found!'

Her brother followed her and she led him to a lonely

part of the garden, out of sight of the windows of the castle.

'Look!' she said. 'Just look!'

There, in front of them, close to the ground, was a hole in the yew hedge. It was more suitable for a cat than a child, but they felt sure they could force their way through.

'If we go through now,' said her brother, 'someone will miss us. It will be time for our dinner or time for your music lesson or our parents may want us. Let's get through at night, when no one will miss us. There is a full moon, so we can see our way.'

'Very well,' said his sister.

During the rest of the day they often visited the hole in the hedge to make sure it had not closed up again, as suddenly as it had opened.

That night, when everyone in the castle was asleep, they let themselves out through a side door and hurried to the place. Both were dressed in old clothes and their eyes were bright with excitement.

'I'll go first,' said the boy. 'Then it will be easier for you to follow.'

He began to wriggle through the hole, very slowly as it was hardly big enough. His sister was frightened in case he got stuck in the middle, and could go neither backward nor forward. But she kept quiet, though she was trembling, and at last her brother called in a low voice:

'I'm through. I'm on the other side.'

Then she followed, and did not find it so difficult, as her brother had forced a way first and she was a little smaller than he. After some minutes, she stood beside him on the far side of the hedge.

They found themselves on smooth, green turf, like velvet,

with some trees forming a circle. Inside this circle some people in green were dancing. They had golden hair, and the women wore long green robes. The men wore green suits. They danced so lightly that their bare feet did not even flatten the grass. Every now and then one of the dancers beckoned to the children to join them.

A squirrel sitting on a branch above their heads whispered:

'It's quite safe to join in the dance, but never accept a bite of food or a sip of drink. Never, however hungry or thirsty you may be.'

Then the children noticed a table set with dishes of little cakes, and jugs of some honey-coloured drink. The dancers sometimes paused to eat a little cake, or pour out a glass of the honey-coloured drink.

Next time one of the people in green beckoned, the children came forward and joined in the dance. Their hands were held by cool, thin fingers and they felt as light as thistledown as they danced. A group of fiddlers made the music, and though the dances were new to them, the children found they could join in perfectly. They made no mistakes.

When the dawn came and the cock crowed, the dancers vanished with the fiddlers and table of refreshments. The children suddenly felt sleepy and crept back through the hedge and hurried into their beds. They fell asleep at once.

Later that day it semed like a dream that they had danced all night and they were not in the least tired or sleepy. That night they went to the dance again, and the next night, and the next. They could not keep away from the dancers in green. The music of the fiddles was so gay and lively, and the people were so friendly. Every time the cock crowed and they went back to their beds, they began to look forward to the following night.

Then, one very hot night, the boy was tempted to have a drink, though his sister begged him not to, and reminded him of the squirrel's warning. But he grew hotter and hotter, and watching the other dancers drinking the honey drink was more than he could bear.

'I must have one sip,' he said. 'I'll just moisten my lips.'

Before his sister could stop him, he broke from the dance, went to the table, and lifted a glass of the honey drink to his mouth. It was so delicious that first he sipped, and then he drank deeply. At once his clothes changed to a green suit like the clothes of the other dancers, and his hair shone like gold. When the cock crowed, he vanished with the rest, and his sister was left alone, with tears streaming down her cheeks.

She woke her father and mother and told them what had happened, but they did not believe her, especially as they could not find the hole in the hedge for themselves. They said she had been dreaming. When they found their son had disappeared they thought he had been stolen and they offered a reward for his return. Their servants rode far and wide over the countryside seeking for him, and all was bustle and confusion.

That night the little girl went through the hole in the hedge again. Her heart was too heavy for dancing, but her feet were as light as ever, and she longed for a glimpse of her brother. When she saw him in his green suit, with his shining golden hair, she grasped his hand and begged him to come home with her. But he looked at her with puzzled eyes and drew away.

'Who are you?' he asked. 'I have never seen you before.'

When the dancers vanished at cock crow, she could not keep back her tears. Then she heard a friendly little voice above her head. It was the squirrel.

'All is not lost,' said the squirrel. 'Do just what I tell you and you may yet get your brother back. When you join the dancers next time, take some iron with you, and some dew from a white rose. Throw the iron into the ring of dancers – they fear iron above all things – and dab the dew on your brother's forehead. Then he will turn back into his own form, and the spell will be broken.'

That night, the girl took some iron nails in her pocket,

and gathered some drops of dew from a white rose in a bottle which she wrapped in her handkerchief. The squirrel had warned her not to try to break the spell at once, but to join in the dancing first.

As she danced, the nails clinked together in her pocket.

'What is that sound?' said one of the dancers.

'It is the buckle of my shoe jingling,' she replied.

Later on the nails clinked again.

'What is that sound?' said another of the dancers.

'It is my shoe squeaking,' she replied.

She waited till she was dancing close to her brother, who looked at her with unseeing eyes, then she suddenly flung the nails into the middle of the ring, and then dabbed the dew on his forehead. At once the dancers in green shrieked and vanished, and her brother changed back into his old form.

'Let us go home now,' she said. 'It is time.' And they crept through the hole in the hedge and into their beds.

There were great rejoicings when their father and mother found their son had returned. As he was unable to say where he had been, they decided a spell had been laid on him, and somehow the spell had been broken.

For several nights the children stayed at home, too glad to be together again to risk being parted, but after a week or so they began to long for the music and the dancing. Also they wanted to thank the kind squirrel for his help. So once more they quietly left the castle by the side door, and crept to the yew hedge.

But the hole had closed up. There was not space enough left for a mouse to get through. So they went back to bed.

They never forgot the dancers in green, and the boy never forgot the taste of the delicious honey drink. But in time they could not remember the tune the fiddlers played, however hard they tried.

Both children grew up to be famous dancers, lighter of foot than anyone else, and they never tired even if they danced all night.

Sea-Mew

ANDREW always liked to read stories about pirates and often wished he could be one himself. So when the chance came, he ran away from home and became a cabin boy on a pirate ship.

It was a real pirate ship and the flag had a skull and cross-bones on it. The pirates mostly wore gold ear-rings, and big, black boots, and had pistols stuck in their belts. They spoke in deep, gruff voices and spent hours and hours looking at maps on tattered bits of paper. These were supposed to show islands where treasure was buried.

Andrew soon got tired of being a pirates' cabin boy. The pirates were kind and often played noughts and crosses with him, though they were upset when he won.

But Andrew's duties were very boring. He had to wash the decks, and make the Captain's bed, and polish his sea-boots, and coil up bits of rope into neat coils.

Every now and then the ship, *The Golden Vanity*, stopped at some island, and a map was got out, and the Captain and the First Mate decided where to dig. Andrew dug as well, but he was small, and the spade was big, and he was usually told to go away and play.

There was no one to play with, of course, but he chased the monkeys, and shouted at the parrots, and picked up shells on the beach. Then he played in the sand and made castles and canals and dug-outs, just as you do.

Somehow, there was always something wrong about the maps. Or else the pirates did not understand them properly.

The hole grew deeper. The pirates grew hotter. The First Mate got angrier. And the Captain lost his temper.

'Shiver my timbers!' he shouted. 'What a pack of ninnies you are!' and he picked up a spade and dug too. But they never dug up anything worth having. No gold or silver or treasure.

Sometimes they met another ship and then they fired their old, rusty cannon to frighten her crew, and went on board waving their pistols. The pistols were so old that they would not fire, but the pirates never needed to fire them. Just to point them was enough. Then they went through the ship from stem to stern, but they never found any treasure. So they departed with anything that took their fancy, such as a new pair of boots, or a cushion for the Captain's cabin.

But one day they came across a very strange ship indeed. The mast was broken right off. The sails were torn to shreds. It was a wreck, except that it still floated.

'That must have been a terrible storm to snap off a mast,' said one of the pirates.

'It was that capful of wind we had last week,' said the Captain. '*The Golden Vanity* is a strong ship, but a weaker one would have felt it badly.'

'Do let's go on board,' said Andrew.

' 'Tisn't likely they left anything behind that's worth having when they took to the boats,' said the First Mate.

'I think they left everything behind,' said Andrew. 'The poor sailors thought the ship was sinking, and they just dropped all they had, tumbled into the boats, and rowed for their lives.'

'There's something in what the boy says,' said the Captain.

So they went on board the wreck. The sailors did not find much, but Andrew found something far better than gold or silver. He heard a faint me-ow, and looked down and saw a thin little black cat. He took her up in his arms, and the me-ow changed to a deep, contented purr. Andrew was not sure that the pirate cook would welcome what he called 'another mouth to feed', so he stuffed pussy up the front of his jersey, where she kept still and quiet.

Once back on *The Golden Vanity* it was impossible to hide her. When the pirates lined up for their grog, and Andrew took his place last for his cocoa, he took his mug and said boldly:

'Milk for the ship's cat, please sir.'

'Milk for who?' said the cook.

'Milk for the ship's cat, please sir. Very good mouser, she is. Very good mouser indeed.'

So the cook opened a tin of milk, poured it into a bowl, and the cat settled down to lap till the very last drop.

Then she spent some time cleaning her whiskers and washing her face.

Life on *The Golden Vanity* was now much more interesting for Andrew. Whenever he was not busy, he played with his cat whom he called Sea-Mew, though she only mewed when she was hungry. Every time she went into the hold, she came out with a mouse in her mouth, and laid it at Andrew's feet. He always showed it to the cook who now took more interest in Sea-Mew. He added chunks of bully beef to the tinned milk. Sea-Mew grew fatter, and her eyes greener, and her fur sleeker. She was now a very fine cat indeed.

When Andrew first found Sea-Mew, he noticed that she had a silver disc hanging from a chain round her neck. As

she grew, the chain got tight and he had to ask the kindest of the pirates, a man named Scarface, to make it longer. The scar on his face was made by falling out of his pram when he was a baby, but it seemed a good name for a pirate. Scarface added a bit of chain very neatly, and Sea-Mew was comfortable again.

On the silver disc there was a shape like this △ with a dot in the corner like this △ Andrew often wondered what it was. Surely it had some meaning? But what could it be?

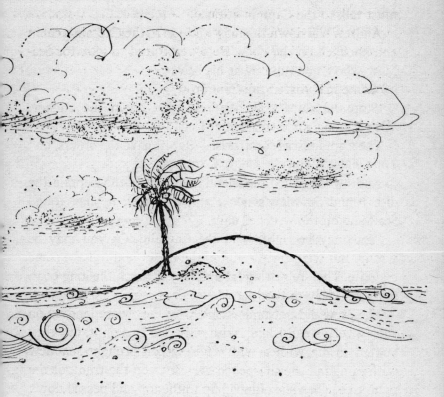

'You'd tell me if you could, wouldn't you?' he said to Sea-Mew, as they swung together in his hammock.

'Purr! Purr!' said Sea-Mew, which was as good as saying: 'I would. I would.'

A few days later, Andrew climbed the mast to look around. At first there was just blue sea. Then a tiny little island with three corners could be seen, with one palm tree at one corner. At once Andrew thought of Sea-Mew's disc. Could the shape be the island, and the single palm tree the dot? Supposing it were. Supposing it were really a map. Supposing there was treasure buried under the palm tree? He must talk to the Captain at once.

Andrew slid down the mast and ran to the Captain's cabin and knocked on the door. He did not need to look for Sea-Mew who came running at his heels.

'Come in!' roared the Captain.

'Stop the ship!' said Andrew. 'Let down the anchor. We've found some treasure at last.'

The Captain was so surprised that he gave the orders, and *The Golden Vanity* came to a stop.

Andrew described the island and showed the Captain the disc round Sea-Mew's neck, and told how he had found Sea-Mew on the wrecked ship.

'You may be right,' said the Captain. 'Or you may be wrong. But we'll try. It will do the crew good to have some exercise. They're getting fat and lazy. Launch the long boat, and let's away to the island.'

The crew did not understand why they were landing on such a very small island, with only one tree on it, but they started to dig with a will. Andrew had brought Sea-Mew with him, and she sharpened her claws on the trunk of the palm tree. Then she climbed up to the top and peered down at them through the leaves.

Soon their spades struck metal and a heavy, iron chest was dragged out of the sand, so heavy that even the Captain had to help to lift it.

Someone had to row back to *The Golden Vanity* for a hammer and chisel, and at last the lid was lifted.

A great big 'Ah!' of delight went up as they saw what was within. The chest was packed solid with golden coins.

'We can all retire,' said the Captain.

'We can live on shore and have homes of our own,' said the crew.

'I can have a new set of saucepans and can keep an hotel at some seaside place,' said the cook.

'What about me?' said Andrew, with Sea-Mew in his arms.

'You can work at my hotel,' said the cook.

'But I want to go home,' said Andrew, bursting into tears. 'I want to live with my father and mother again. I've been a cabin boy long enough.'

Everyone was very nice to him and tried to comfort him. The Captain patted him on the shoulder and said:

'Quite right, my boy. Home is the best place for you.'

'He was not old enough to wash the decks properly,' said the First Mate.

'Or to clean the saucepans,' said the cook.

'Or to polish my sea-boots,' said the Captain.

'Or to coil rope neatly,' said Scarface.

'Take this,' said the Captain, pushing a handful of gold into Andrew's hands. 'We should never have found the treasure without your help.'

They pulled down the flag with the skull and cross-bones, and made for the nearest port, where Andrew bought a leather bag to keep his gold in. He found he was so rich that he could hire an aeroplane to fly himself and Sea-Mew home.

There was gold enough to give his father and mother a nice present; and then Andrew went back to school, because he had decided on the flight home to be a pilot when he grew up; and pilots must learn lessons and pass exams.

Sea-Mew got even fatter on fresh cow's milk which she liked better than the tinned kind.

The Magic Shilling

A LITTLE boy and his little white dog were walking along a snowy road. The boy was named Ben and his dog was Stumpy. It was easy to see Ben because he had a red woollen cap on and a long red woollen scarf and red woollen mittens. But it was hard to see Stumpy because he was white and so was the snow. Sometimes he sank into a drift and had to bark 'Bow-wow! Bow-wow-wow!' till Ben looked back and pulled him out.

Soon they came to a hut by the roadside. An old, old woman lived in the hut. She was trying to clear a path from her door to the gate. But she was not strong enough. She could not move the deep snow.

'I'll do it for you,' said Ben. 'Give me the spade and the broom.'

'Thank you,' said the old woman. 'I'll nip back to the fire and warm myself while you work.'

The spade was too big and heavy for Ben, but he did his best to clear a path, and Stumpy helped by scraping with his paws. Then Ben knocked on the door.

'I've cleared a path,' he said.

'Thank you,' said the old woman. 'Will you chop some wood while you are here?'

So Ben chopped some wood.

When he knocked on the door and said he had chopped the wood, the old woman said:

'Thank you. Will you fetch some potatoes from the shed while you are here?'

So Ben fetched some potatoes.

When he knocked on the door and said he had fetched the potatoes, the old woman said:

'Will you peel them while you are here?'

Ben peeled the potatoes. So it went on all day. He swept the hearth, and washed the floor, and shook the feather bed, and did all kinds of jobs.

When it was getting dark and the sun was setting like a red ball of fire, the old woman said:

'Thank you. You may go now. Here is a shilling for you, and a bone for your dog. But don't give it to him till you are both at home.'

So Ben went home, watching the red glow of the sun on the snow. He was happy with his silver money in his pocket. Stumpy was happy too because he could smell the bone and knew it was for him.

When they got home, Stumpy chewed his meaty bone and then buried what was left in the snow, and Ben planned what to do with his shilling. There was something in the village shop that he wanted to buy.

The next day Ben went to the shop and the thing he wanted was still there. It was a wooden horse and cart, with a smiling boy on the driving seat. Ben felt as if he were the smiling boy when he played with it.

During the day Stumpy dug up his bone and found there was plenty of meat on it still. So he had another meal off it.

The next day Ben was looking in the shop window when he saw a toy stable.

'I should like that for my horse,' he thought. Just then he put his hand in his pocket and his fingers felt something thin and round. It was another silver shilling. How could it have got there? He was sure the old woman had only given him

one shilling. Still, he thought he would spend it, and he bought the stable.

When he got home, Stumpy dug up his bone again and there was still meat on it. So he had another good meal off it.

The next day Ben found another shilling in his pocket. He did not understand where it came from, but there it was. This time be bought a doll for his sister. When he brought the doll home he saw that Stumpy had dug his bone up again and was chewing great pieces of meat off it.

So it went on. Every day Ben found another shilling in his pocket, and every day Stumpy found more meat on his bone. Sometimes Ben bought things for himself, and sometimes for his father and mother and sister.

The other boys in the village found out about the shilling and tried to take it, but they never managed to get it. Stumpy guarded his master so well, and snapped and growled. He turned from a meek little dog into a raging fury.

One day a poor, half-starved dog came by and begged for a bite of the meaty bone. He whined and begged for just one bite. But Stumpy drove him away. The next day, when he dug up his bone, it was quite bare. Not a shred of meat was left on it. So that was the end of the magic bone.

Ben kept his magic shilling for more than a year, till one day a little beggar girl asked him for a penny. He knew he could have changed the shilling into twelve pennies and given her one, but he was playing with his horse and cart and did not want to be disturbed. So he said:

'Go away! I've nothing for you!'

From that moment the shilling never came back into his pocket, never again.

More Bristles from the Witch's Broom

NOT every child is lucky enough to know a witch. Robert
and his friend Polly were specially lucky to know Mrs Crabapple, who was not only a witch, but lived in their own
village, and was a friend of theirs. Her house was called *The
Spider's Web*. They often called to see her, and always found
her doing something interesting. Sometimes she was brew-
ing herbs in her cauldron, or reading her Spell Books aloud
to the cat. If she was doing a messy job, the broomstick leapt
from its corner and swept the floor, without even being
asked.

Although Mrs Crabapple had two friends, Robert and
Polly, she felt hurt that the ladies in the village never called
to see her.

'Why does no one ask me out to tea?' she asked the
children.

They did not like to say it was because she was so queer,
and people wondered why she wandered about at night, and
talked to her cat, and had a garden full of nettles and
thistles.

'Perhaps you ought to give a party,' suggested Polly.
'When people move into a new house they give a party
called a house-warming. They ask all their neighbours and
give them tea and cakes and they all get to know each
other.'

'A wonderful idea,' beamed Mrs Crabapple. 'I'll have a
house-warming next week and ask everyone in the village.'

Mrs Crabapple wrote the invitations with a goose-quill

dipped in home-made purple ink, and bought a recipe book and some cake tins. She did not think much of the recipes which contained, in her opinion, far too much sugar. So she added her favourite flavourings which were vinegar, spice, lemon juice, and ground acorns.

She spent the morning before the party baking parsley pancakes which she felt sure would be a treat. After dinner, she set out the plates of good things, and put on her best dress which was black satin embroidered with red snakes and green frogs. She scented her handkerchief with peppermint, and sat down and waited for the guests to arrive.

At four o'clock the gate began to squeak as the ladies arrived and picked their way through the tangle of weeds. Although Mrs Crabapple was all smiles and sweetness, the party went badly from the start. Her icy cold handshake made the guests shiver, and they felt uncomfortable on the wooden chairs without cushions and the stools without backs, which was all there was to sit on.

Mrs Crabapple made the tea from her cauldron and the ladies noticed that she put nettles, not tea-leaves, in the pot. The bitter flavour of the cakes drew up their mouths, and the famous parsley pancakes were tough and peculiar. To make matters worse, no one seemed to want to talk. At last one lady remarked:

'Good weather we're having.'

'Yes indeed,' agreed several others.

'It won't last,' said Mrs Crabapple firmly. 'It was the viper's moon last night, and she was misty. A bad sign. Rain before morning.'

No one had heard of the viper's moon and they did not like the sound of it.

'I am so troubled by mice in the kitchen,' began another

lady. 'My cat doesn't keep them off at all. Can anyone help me?'

. 'I never have any trouble with mice,' said Mrs Crabapple cheerfully. 'Never have had any. I leave a good lump of cheese on the hearth for them, and a few crusts, and they eat them up and never go near the larder. Treat mice well and they'll treat *you* well.'

By this time the visitors were longing to get home. The hard chairs and the strange food and Mrs Crabapple's even stranger ideas had upset them. The house was haunted by a number of small creatures which were not pleasant and the ladies were kept busy getting spiders out of their hair and beetles from their sleeves. They had to lift their feet while a pet toad hopped slowly across the floor, and they jumped each time the broom sprang from its corner to sweep up a stray crumb someone had dropped.

At last they gabbled their thanks, endured another icy handshake, and made off as fast they could. They had plenty to talk about on the way home.

'What could she have put in those dreadful pancakes?'

'I tasted mint and vinegar –'

'And there was a piece of bone in mine.'

'There's no doubt about her being a witch.'

'Viper's moon, indeed!'

'That cat stared and stared at me till I didn't know where to look.'

When Robert and Polly ran to *The Spider's Web* to hear about the party, they found Mrs Crabapple washing up with tears splashing into the water. She told them how no one had liked the food or the pet toad or anything else. They saw what a failure the house-warming had been and they tried to comfort her by telling her how much cleverer she was than most people and they even finished up the parsley pancakes to please her. Polly's last words were:

'You ought to show people a sample of your magic. Then they'd understand what a wonderful person you are. They just don't know half the things you can do.'

Mrs Crabapple thought over these words and the next day she sent each of her guests a tiny posy of flowers with a card on which was written:

With Mrs Crabapple's Compliments

The posies were simple enough, a few wild flowers and a spray of fern, but when days passed and they did not fade, and weeks passed and they did not fade, the guests understood that this was a sign of Mrs Crabapple's powers.

Some of the posies were stitched on to hats or pinned on dresses. Some were kept in water. Some were kept dry. But all stayed fresh and sweet. Not a leaf or a petal fell.

After this, the village folk were more friendly. They taught the boys to take their caps off to Mrs Crabapple and they gave her jars of home-made jam. She found the jam too sweet and sickly and added it to the mice's supper on the hearth. Many a mouse sat up half the night, cleaning his sticky whiskers.

People in trouble began to slip round to *The Spider's Web* for advice, and often a lost article was found or an illness cured after one of the spell books had been consulted. Soon everyone was saying, 'Whatever did we do before we had a witch in the village? I can't think how we managed, can you?'

Pom-Pom and the Ju-ju Man

POM-POM was a little black boy and he lived in a hut with mud walls and a roof thatched with leaves. He was fat and round and Pom-Pom was a suitable name for him.

Pom-Pom had a kind father and mother. He had a kind grandfather and grandmother. He had many kind uncles and aunts, and cousins. All these people loved him and took care of him. But even so there were not enough of them to look after him properly. He was always getting into trouble.

If he was left alone for just one minute, he played with the fire or upset the water pot or pricked himself on one of his father's arrows. Even when it was dinner-time and a bowl of stew was put in front of him, he couldn't manage to eat it nicely. He gobbled and gobbled so fast that he sometimes had a pain afterwards, or was sick.

One day, Pom-Pom's mother was busy in the garden. His father was away fishing. His grandfather and grandmother were spring-cleaning their hut, and all his other relations had jobs they wanted to do. No one had time to look after such a naughty little boy as Pom-Pom.

So his mother took a long rope made of creeper and tied one end round Pom-Pom's waist, and the other to a tree. It was a very long rope and he could run about and play, but he could not reach the fire or go inside the hut and get into mischief.

'Here are your toys,' said his mother, giving him some sticks and pebbles and his bamboo pipe. 'If you feel hot, you can lie down in the shade of the tree. I've left a jar of water in case you are thirsty. I shall be back by dinner-time. Good-bye, and be good.'

At first Pom-Pom didn't really believe that he could be left alone, tied to a tree like a cow or a goat, but when his mother walked off with her basket on her head, and her hoe over her shoulder, he knew that it was true. He really *was* alone, though he could see his grandparents in the distance, turning out their hut, and some of his relations busy with this and that.

First he screamed. He screamed and screamed till his throat hurt.

Then he stamped his feet and clenched his fists and made ugly faces.

Then he cried till his tears made wet rivers down his cheeks.

Then he whimpered and grizzled.

While he was deciding what to do next, the Ju-ju man came into sight. He lived in a large hut that stood all by itself, just outside the village, and he made magic. Pom-Pom had often been told to be very, very careful if he met the Ju-ju man, but he forgot what he had been told when the Ju-ju man said:

'Why have you been crying, little black boy?'

'Because I am tied up like a goat,' said Pom-Pom.

'If I let you free,' said the Ju-ju man, 'will you come with me to my hut and be my servant?'

'Yes, yes, indeed I will,' said Pom-Pom. 'Set me free and I'll do anything!'

So the Ju-ju man undid the rope and Pom-Pom was free. He felt happy and important walking along beside the Ju-ju man, who was wearing a very grand head-dress made of feathers, and several necklaces made of teeth.

When they reached the hut, Pom-Pom could hardly believe his eyes. It was so large and contained so many wonderful things. The walls were hung with beads and spears and monkeys' tails and other curious objects. There were clay jars in a row with leaves tied over the top. These held the Ju-ju man's magic medicines.

'I will tell you what your duties are,' said the Ju-ju man. 'Listen carefully because I don't want to have to tell you twice.'

Pom-Pom had already forgotten that he was now a servant, and he did not like the idea of having duties to do. But he was a little afraid of the Ju-ju man, who was tall and thin and had a voice that crackled. So he listened carefully.

'You must sweep my floor every day with the broom.'

Pom-Pom saw that the broom was made of thin twigs tied together.

'You must dust all my belongings, especially my clay jars.'

Pom-Pom saw that there was a little whisk made of feathers to dust with.

'You must see that my pot of broth doesn't boil over.'

Pom-Pom saw that there was a long wooden spoon, nearly as tall as himself, with which to stir the broth.

'You must come when I call, and sit very still and quiet when I am thinking. Oh, and when I'm asleep, you must keep the flies away with a fan.'

Pom-Pom saw that the fan was a cool, green leaf with a stalk for a handle. He felt sad. He knew he was going to be very, very busy indeed, with all these jobs to do.

The next morning early, Pom-Pom's mother came to the door of the hut.

'What do you want?' asked the Ju-ju man, who was used to people coming to him for advice.

'I want Pom-Pom,' said Pom-Pom's mother.

'You can't have him,' said the Ju-ju man, 'because he belongs to me now. He is my servant.'

'Do you know how to look after a little boy?' asked Pom-Pom's mother. 'Can you wash him every day?'

'No,' said the Ju-ju man.

'Can you comb his hair which is always full of tangles?'

'No,' said the Ju-ju man.

'Can you see to him when he is sick?'

'No,' said the Ju-ju man.

'Can you sing him to sleep if he wakes in the night after a bad dream?'

'No, no, indeed I can't,' said the Ju-ju man.

It seemed as if Pom-Pom wouldn't have to be a servant after all, if he needed all this looking after. But the Ju-ju man soon had another idea.

'You can come every day and look after Pom-Pom,' he said to Pom-Pom's mother. 'When he is washed and combed and all the rest of it, then he can work. I go out on business soon after sunrise and I am not back till sunset. I shall expect my hut to be clean and tidy when I return.'

So every morning when the Ju-ju man went off into the forest on business, Pom-Pom's mother came. She soon tidied him and washed him, and she had time to do all his work as well, and even made the broth. When the Ju-ju man came back at sunset, everything was neat and shining, and Pom-Pom was neat and shining too. The Ju-ju man thought that Pom-Pom had done all the work himself, and he sometimes patted him on the head and said, 'Good boy!' or gave him a handful of dates as a treat.

But one day the Ju-ju man came home early because there was a thunderstorm, and he found Pom-Pom curled up on his best blanket, playing with his precious medicine jars, while Pom-Pom's mother swept and dusted and cooked.

The Ju-ju man was very angry.

'So this is what happens when I'm away!' he shouted. 'My servant sits on my best blanket doing nothing while his mother works. Why, you're no more use than a tortoise. In fact you'd be more useful as a tortoise,' and he dipped his fingers in one of his medicine jars and sprinkled some white powder among Pom-Pom's curls.

At once Pom-Pom began to shrink. His head became smooth and flat and scaly. His arms and legs shrivelled till they were small and wrinkled. His back shrank into a hard, brown shell marked into faint squares. He was a tortoise, a real tortoise, with a neat little tail at one end, and a nose with two tiny holes to breathe through at the other.

'You can eat the crumbs I drop to save sweeping the floor,' said the Ju-ju man, 'and you can be my footstool if my feet ache. If you are any more trouble, I shall turn you into something quite, quite useless and forget about you; perhaps a blade of grass or a puff of smoke.'

Pom-Pom's mother begged and pleaded with him to be a good tortoise. 'At least you can see and hear and speak,' she said to him, 'and you can creep, too. If you were a blade of grass or a puff of smoke I might lose sight of you. You would be gone for ever.'

So Pom-Pom tried to be good. If the Ju-ju man dropped any crumbs, he ate them up, and if the Ju-ju man's feet ached and he needed a footstool, Pom-Pom kept very still. But once or twice he crept away because he had cramp, or just because he was bored, and if the Ju-ju man had waked

up and noticed his stool was gone, that might have been the end of Pom-Pom.

Pom-Pom's mother never gave up hope of changing her son back into a boy. One day she said to the Ju-ju man:

'Oh mighty Ju-ju man. I have a question to ask.'

'What is it?' asked the Ju-ju man.

'I hardly like to ask it because it is so difficult,' said Pom-Pom's mother.

'No question is too difficult for me,' said the Ju-ju man, who was a great boaster. 'Ask me and I will answer.'

'How can you make someone tell you a secret?'

'Ha! Ha!' laughed the Ju-ju man. 'That's very easy indeed. I don't deny that some people would find it difficult, but it's easy to me. Why, you wait till the person is asleep and squeeze his little finger gently. Then whatever you ask, he will answer truly.'

'Which little finger?' asked Pom-Pom's mother. 'The one on the left hand, or on the right?'

'The left, of course. Now don't ask me any more questions.'

Pom-Pom's mother could hardly wait for the Ju-ju man to go to sleep that night. Then she tip-toed to his side, took hold of the little finger of his left hand, and squeezed it gently. Then she whispered in his ear:

'How can I turn a tortoise into a little boy?'

'Rub his shell with pink pepper,' said the Ju-ju man sleepily.

Pom-Pom's mother began opening each of the clay jars in turn, though the night was so dark that she could hardly see what was inside. But when she began sneezing and sneezing and sneezing, she knew she had found the pepper, and she could only hope it was the right colour. She took a pinch and rubbed it all over Pom-Pom's shell.

Slowly his shell became soft and smooth and warm. His front legs grew into long, thin, black arms, and his back legs into long, thin, black legs. His narrow head grew round and curls sprouted. His crack of a mouth stretched into a wide smile showing two rows of white teeth.

'My own dear Pom-Pom!' cried his mother.

'My own dear mother!' cried Pom-Pom, and they hugged each other. Then, very quietly, they crept out of the large hut and back to their own, cosy small one.

The next day, when Pom-Pom's mother was combing his tangly hair, the comb scraped on something hard and rough. It was a tiny square of scaly tortoise skin left among his curls. The pink pepper had not been rubbed on this one spot.

'It will remind you of what happened when the Ju-ju man turned you into a tortoise,' said his mother. 'It will remind you to be good and to do what you are told.'

'Yes, Mother,' said Pom-Pom, feeling the rough bit with his finger.

He went off to play with the other children in the village. He allowed them to feel his special bit of tortoise skin if they gave him something nice to eat, nuts or dates or berries. As *all* the children wanted to feel his head, and they *all* brought him something to eat, he was – can you guess? Yes, he was very sick indeed and he had to lie in the shade with a cool leaf on his head, while his mother sang to him.

Three Gold Coins

THERE was once a shepherd lad who kept his sheep on the green slopes surrounding a little village. He had no father or mother, and he lived in a hut with an old shepherd who had brought him up since his parents died.

As he grew from boyhood to manhood, he sometimes thought he would like to see the world and to visit some large city where crowds of people thronged the streets, and the shops were filled with marvellous things for sale. But he had not the heart to leave the good old man who had shown him such kindness, and even if he had run away to the city, he had no money to spend there.

Every morning, when the young shepherd left his hut, he met a goosegirl taking her flock of snow-white geese on to the village green. The geese looked at him and his dog Flush with dark, narrow eyes, and sometimes bent their long necks and hissed. But the boy took no notice of the geese. He gazed, instead, at the goosegirl who had two yellow plaits down her back and a shy, but friendly, smile.

At first the shepherd and the goosegirl just smiled at each other. Then they wished each other good morning. Then they stopped for a chat. After a time, Flush lay down for a nap when he saw the flock of geese approaching, and even the restless geese stopped waddling along and began to eat the grass by the roadside. Both dog and birds knew that it would be a long while before their master and mistress went on their separate ways.

The shepherd and the goosegirl fell in love and when the

first leaves fell from the trees, the shepherd asked the girl's father if they might be married in the spring.

'I can't allow my daughter to marry a poor shepherd,' said the father angrily. 'How will you find a house fit for her to live in? How will you buy clothes suitable for her to wear and good food for her to eat? When you can show me three gold coins you have saved, and a house to live in, I will consider giving my permission.'

This was a great blow. The shepherd could never hope to save three gold coins, or to buy a house. The next day it was almost noon before the sheep saw their shepherd or the geese arrived at the village green, there was so much to be discussed by their master and mistress.

When the old man heard the story he said: 'Go to the city, my boy, and get as good a job as you can. Who knows, when the spring comes you may have earned your gold coins. I will keep the sheep till you return, old and feeble though I am.'

The young man did not like leaving his dear old friend and foster father to keep the sheep in the bitter winter weather, but the goosegirl promised to knit the old man a warm waistcoat and muffler, and to take him a hot dinner every Sunday. So the boy made up his mind to leave for the city the very next day. He said good-bye to the goosegirl, patted his dog Flush, and asked the old man for his blessing, and for any good advice that might help him. The old man blessed him and gave him this advice. 'Work hard. Speak the truth. Help any living thing in trouble.'

The young man set out towards the city which was three days' journey from the village. On the first day he strode on quickly, being fresh and full of hope. He stopped only once, to free a wild goose which had been caught in a snare set by a fowler. As the goose stretched her wings, thankful to be free, she fixed her dark eyes on the boy's face and said:

'Thank you, young man. You have saved my life. Take this feather and keep it carefully. It may come in useful one day,' and she shook a pure white feather from her wing. The young man put it safely inside his jacket and the goose flew off to join her companions.

On the second day, the young man strode on almost as quickly, singing as he went. He stopped only once to rescue a baby squirrel which had fallen from its drey into a prickly holly bush. He freed it gently, and its mother took it in her mouth and ran nimbly up the beech tree to her nest. Then, as he moved away, she ran after him and said:

'Thank you, young man. You have saved my child's life. Take this fir cone and keep it carefully. It may come in useful one day,' and she laid a brown, shining fir cone at his feet. He put it safely in his pocket, and the squirrel ran back to her children.

On the third day the young man was getting foot-sore, but he still strode along at a smart pace, glad to see the faint outline of the city's towers and spires in the distance. He stopped only once to save a ladybird who was drowning in a puddle of water. He skimmed her out with a leaf and was going to put her on a sunny stone to dry, when she spoke to him and said:

'Thank you, young man. You have saved my life. If you take me with you on your travels, I may come in useful one day.'

So the young man picked a flower and a leaf and stuck them in his button-hole, and the ladybird settled herself in the centre of the flower. Before the sun had set, they had reached the city, and before the moon had risen, the young man had hired himself to a wise doctor to make a neat copy of the book he was writing. For though the young man was poor, he had been taught by the village schoolmaster to write a clear, flowing hand.

Now this wise doctor, though very learned, was a miser and hated to part with his money. He offered his new clerk a gold coin when the book was finished, but whenever the end was in sight, he gave the boy yet another bundle of scrawled, scribbled sheets to copy neatly. At last the young man protested that the task was impossible because the book had no ending, and he would like to leave and find another job. This did not suit the old miser who had never before had such a good, careful clerk who worked such long hours and never made a mistake.

'I'll make a bargain with you,' he said, handing over a further pile of pages. 'Copy these neatly by sunrise tomorrow and I'll pay you a gold coin. But if you fail, you will have to leave with no wages.'

The young man had no choice but to agree and he set to work on this last task, not stopping for food or drink or rest. He found that the pages he had to copy were closely written on both sides, with many crossings-out and blots, and the task seemed impossible, especially when twilight fell and the mean old doctor only allowed him the light of one poor candle to work by.

As his pen toiled over the page, and he strained his eyes to read the crabbed writing, a voice said to him: 'Use me. I can help you.' It was the goosefeather speaking from inside his jacket. He took it out, examined it carefully, and cut the end into a point for writing. Then he dipped his new quill pen into the ink and went on with his copying.

To his amazement, the quill pen flew across the paper so fast that he could hardly keep a grip on it, leaving behind line after line of clear, even writing. Before the sun rose, the young man was able to hand his master a fair copy of every page.

The miser was angry to find that the task he had thought imposible had been faultlessly carried out. He could only throw a gold coin into the street and say to the young man : 'Go and pick up your wages and never come back.' The young man was only too pleased to snatch up the coin and disappear as fast as his legs would carry him.

The gold coin he tied in one corner of his best handkerchief.

Before the day passed, he had hired himself to a goldsmith who promised him a golden coin if he could keep the furnace hot and glowing, day and night, for a week. This sounded an easy task, and the young man gladly accepted it. All day long he tended the furnace, stoking it when necessary and blowing it with the bellows till it glowed white hot. At night he woke several times and got up from his bed on the floor in the corner, to see if it needed attention.

But as the days went by, he grew sleepier and sleepier, and he was so tired when he lay down at night that he found it almost impossible to wake himself up and see to the furnace. Twice he did not wake till it was almost light and the furnace was so low that he was only able to revive it after very energetic work with the bellows.

When the fifth night came, and there were still two nights more, he was almost ill with weariness. He dared not lie on his bed, hard though it was, as he knew he would fall asleep directly. So he tried to rest leaning against the wall. Suddenly, as he swayed with sleepiness, a voice said to him: 'Use me. I can help you.' It was the fir cone the squirrel had given him, speaking from inside his jacket pocket.

'Throw me into the furnace and go to sleep till morning,' said the fir cone. 'All will be well.'

The young man did as he was told, though he did not like throwing the friendly little fir cone into the hot fire, and he lay down on his bed in the corner and fell asleep at once. When morning came, he woke with a start to feel the sun shining on his face, and was relieved to find the furnace clear and glowing.

This continued till the seven days and nights were over, and he asked the goldsmith for his wages. He was paid a gold coin, which he tied into another corner of his handker-chief before hurrying off to look for work somewhere else.

This time, he met a company of strolling actors and found that one of their number had fallen ill, and could not play his part. The leader of the troupe was mad with worry because that very evening they were billed to perform before the King and Queen. He hurried to the young man, held him firmly by the coat, and studied his face and appearance.

'You are just the boy I am looking for,' he cried eagerly. 'Have you a good memory?'

'I don't know,' replied the young man. 'I could remember the faces of each of my flock of sheep and knew if one were missing.'

'That's no help,' said the leader. 'Can you learn by heart?'

'I can but try.'

'Then come with us and I'll show you what you have to do. I want you to play the part of the hero tonight when we act at the palace in front of the King and Queen. If you get through without spoiling the show, I'll give you a gold coin.'

He led the young man to a barn which had been swept and cleaned, sat him down on a bundle of straw, and put a torn and tattered book into his hands.

'I've underlined your part in red,' the actor explained, 'so you can see what you have to learn.'

'But – but there's so much of it,' gasped the young man. 'And such long speeches. I have something to say on almost every page.'

'Don't waste your time complaining. Think of the golden coin that will be yours, and the good supper they'll give us at the palace when the play is over. At tea-time we'll let you try on your costume and we'll run through the play. Good-bye till then. Here's a loaf and cheese and a jug of water.' The actor rushed away, locking the door of the barn behind him.

As the day went on, the young man read and re-read his part, striding up and down the barn, repeating the words aloud. When the time came for the rehearsal, he knew about half his part, and the leader allowed him to read the rest from the book. Then he was left alone again to try to learn the second half.

When the troupe reached the gates of the palace in the evening, he was trembling with fright and his head was aching violently. Suddenly he heard a gentle voice saying, close to his ear: 'Use me. I can help you.' It was the lady-bird who had been living in his buttonhole ever since he rescued her from the puddle. He was thankful he had re-membered to replace the flower when it faded.

'I will whisper the words in your ear if you forget them,'

she went on. 'All my family have very good memories. I shall not fail.'

The young man stopped trembling and his head ceased to throb. He put on his velvet cloak, buckled on his sword and saw, in the mirror, how different and dashing he looked with rouge on his cheeks and false black whiskers. He did not forget to pin his buttonhole safely in position and to notice his tiny helper clinging among the petals.

As the curtains parted, he gave one glance at the audience,

and bowed to the King and Queen, then he began to speak. The words came freely and easily, and if, for a second, he hesitated, the ladybird immediately whispered the forgotten words.

When the play was over, the audience clapped and shouted and the players had to come back upon the stage again and again to bow. The King and Queen were so pleased with the show that they gave each of the actors a golden coin, and as the leader also paid his promised reward, the young man now had four gold coins tied into the four corners of his handkerchief.

He spent one gold coin in the city and bought a wedding ring and a bridal veil of finest lace. Then he set off for his own village. This time, the way seemed short and he was soon opening the door of the hut where he lived with the old man. He noticed that the roof had been newly thatched and the floor swept and the place left clean and tidy.

'You have been like a son to me for many years,' said the old man, as they greeted each other. 'You shall have a son's reward. I am going to spend the last years of my life with my sister, who is lonely and feeble. The flock of sheep are now your own and so is this hut.'

The young man wept to part with his old foster father, but the goosegirl was able to comfort him as they planned their wedding. Her father gave his permission willingly when he heard that they had a place to live in, a flock of sheep and three gold coins.

All the shepherds from far and near came to the wedding and made an archway with their crooks as the bride and bridegroom came out of the church door, the bride's veil blowing like a white cloud and her yellow plaits pinned round her head like a gold crown.

Four Kittens

MINNIE the cat lay in her box under the kitchen table. She was busy with her four new kittens who, though they needed a great deal of sleep, also needed a great deal of washing, and training, and mothering. They had now reached the stage of asking questions, which Minnie answered as best she could. Sometimes, when it was a particularly difficult question, like: 'Why is it dark at night?' she answered sharply:

'You'd better ask your father.'

This led nowhere, as their father took little interest in them, and seldom even visited them.

'Why does the fire eat coal?' asked One, who was the oldest in the family.

'Why is milk good for us?' asked Two.

'Why does Mrs Plum walk on only two legs?' asked Three.

'Why does fish have bones?' asked Four, the youngest.

All these questions and many more, Minnie dealt with patiently.

The kittens were old enough to be taken into the garden on a sunny day, where, as a great treat, they watched Minnie sharpen her claws on the apple tree. Sometimes Minnie climbed a little way up the tree and the kittens longed to do the same, but their claws were not strong enough to get a firm hold yet. They just fell down when they tried.

Lessons went on even when they were in the garden, as

there was so much for the kittens to learn, and not much time for learning. When they could wash themselves properly, and eat fish and liver tidily, and not splash their milk, they would go to new homes. By this time they should have learned that fire is hot. Water wet. That bees and wasps sting. And many other useful things.

After lunch, when the kittens had pleased Minnie by drinking their milk without paddling in the saucer, and eating their fish without choking, Minnie hoped for a short rest.

'Go to sleep, my darlings,' she said to the kittens. 'Then, later on, I will take you into the garden and teach you how to pounce.'

'I don't want to learn to pounce,' said One, who was contrary.

'Then you'll never learn to catch mice,' said Minnie severely, 'and you won't even be able to catch Mrs Plum's ball of wool when it rolls across the floor. All sensible cats can pounce.'

'What is that noise on the ceiling?' asked Two, hearing some thumps above her head.

'It comes from upstairs,' said Minnie. 'Mrs Plum is walking about up there.'

'What is upstairs?' went on Two.

'It is the part of the house where people sleep,' said Minnie, 'and there's a bathroom where water gushes out of taps. A kitten might lose some, or even all, of his nine lives if he fell into a bath of water.'

'What a horrid place!' said Two, shuddering.

'Yes, it's horrid,' agreed Minnie, 'but it has some good points. There are towels hanging on a rail, and it is pleasant to pull them off on to the floor and roll on them. Also there is a deliciously warm cupboard called the airing cupboard. If the door happens to be left open, you can have a sleep there, till you are found, and turned out.

'Now if you go into the bedrooms Mrs Plum is really cross. Grown-up people sleep on beds with warm blankets and eiderdowns, yet they are not willing for cats to have even a corner of them. Except for children, who sometimes take a cat to bed with them, and allow them to creep about under the clothes and play with their toes. I have passed many an enjoyable hour in this way.'

The kittens went on asking questions about the bathroom and bedrooms till at last Minnie said:

'No more questions till we've all had a sleep. Then we'll go out.'

In a few minutes Minnie was fast asleep, and so were Three and Four. But One and Two lay awake, whispering.

'Shall we go upstairs?' said One.

'Yes, let's do that,' said Two.

Both kittens climbed safely out of their box and set off across the kitchen. They went past the fire that ate coal, and past the rug that was warm, and over the red tiled floor that was cool. The door was ajar, and they slipped through into the hall.

When they reached the bottom of the stairs, they looked up. What a long way it looked, up the stairs, and up, and up. They couldn't see the top.

'I'll go first,' said One.

'Don't leave me behind,' said Two, timidly.

Each stair was a climb, but they got better with practice. Half-way up was a small landing where they stopped to get their breath. There was a grandfather clock on the landing. His tick-tock sounded loud and frightening.

'He doesn't like us,' said Two. 'He wants us to go away.'

'Rubbish!' said One. 'He's the same kind of creature as the clock in the kitchen, only much bigger. He tells us when it's time for supper, or time to get up. Mother says he's a friend.'

'He doesn't *sound* like a friend,' said Two. 'Let's go on. I don't like him.'

They scrambled up the next flight of stairs and found they were on the main landing.

'This is the bathroom,' said One. 'I can smell the soap, just as Mother said. And there are the towels on a rail. I shall pull them off and roll on them.'

He ran into the bathroom and as his tiny claws easily hooked themselves into the towels, he managed to pull them off, one by one. Then he rolled on them, enjoying the strange bathroom smell of soap, toothpaste, and bathsalts.

Two was too timid to go into the bathroom. She didn't want to lose any of her nine lives. So she tip-toed along the landing till she came to an open door. In the room was a bed, just as Mother had said. By climbing up a piece of blanket that was hanging down, she managed to get right on top of the bed.

At first she could not find a way in. Then she found an opening near the pillow and squeezed in, and cuddled down.

It was a wonderful bed, far softer than her own bed in the kitchen. She decided to stay there as her short legs ached from their climb up the stairs. She closed her eyes, and before you could say 'mouse trap' she was fast asleep.

Presently there were footsteps coming along the landing. Mrs Plum was on her way downstairs. She poked her head round the open bedroom door, muttered something about 'that's not the way to make a bed', tucked the blanket firmly under all the way round, straightened the quilt, and shut the door.

Two lay quaking inside the bed. The clothes had been tucked in so well by Mrs Plum, that she felt suffocated. She could not remember how she had got in, and she could not find another way out. She cried for help at the top of her voice, but her frantic mews were smothered.

'If I ever get out of here I'll never go upstairs again,' she promised herself.

She knew her mother would find her in the end. She always did. But she hoped she wouldn't be too long. She could hardly breathe, there was so little air.

One heard Mrs Plum coming, and he hid himself under one of the towels he had pulled on to the floor. Mrs Plum walked into the bathroom, picked up a towel and hung it on the rail. Then picked up another and hung that on the rail too. The last towel, in which One was hiding, she bundled into the dirty linen basket, ready for the wash. The towel was so big, and One was so small, that she never knew he was there. She put the lid on the basket, gave a last look round, shut the door, and went on her way.

One was not at all comfortable mixed up with dirty clothes. But he was a brave little kitten and did not waste his breath in mewing. He tried to get free of the towel so as to climb up the side of the basket, but it was too difficult. His claws were caught. He was a prisoner.

One knew what would happen to him. He had often seen Mrs Plum with a sink full of soapy water, squeezing and rinsing and mangling the clothes; then hanging them on the line to dry. Supposing he found himself in a sink full of soapy water, what then? He didn't like the idea of being rinsed and mangled and pegged out to dry.

He tried harder than ever to scramble up the side of the basket.

When Mrs Plum got to the kitchen, she said to Minnie

'Why don't you take the kittens out into the sunshine?'

Minnie heard and understood, and she half opened her eyes in reply. But even through half-open eyes she could see there was something wrong. Something missing. Three and

Four were sleeping peacefully beside her, but there was no sign of One and Two.

Minnie sprang out of the box mewing loudly, looking up at Mrs Plum with gooseberry green eyes. Mrs Plum understood what was wrong, and laid down her knitting.

'We'll find them,' she said. 'Don't fret.'

Minnie looked at the backdoor which was shut. Then at the door into the hall which was open. She ran through this, sniffing eagerly at the hall rug.

With a hasty, 'Don't dare to move till I come back' to Three and Four, she went on her way, letting her nose guide her. Yes, they had been this way, and upstairs, past the clock, and up the next flight. On the landing she paused and listened. All the doors were shut. Then she ran to the bathroom door and began to scratch on it. Her ears had caught the faint sound of One scrabbling in the clothes-basket.

Mrs Plum opened the door and in a minute One was released, with white threads of towel still hanging from his claws.

Two's mews were too muffled for Mrs Plum to hear, but Minnie caught the tiny sound and scratched at the bedroom door. Then Mrs Plum turned back the bedclothes and there was Two, her fur damp with heat, and all rubbed up the wrong way. She was in such a state that even with Minnie licking her, she could not stop crying.

Mrs Plum carried the kittens downstairs and laid them in the empty box, empty because Three and Four had both got into mischief. Three was climbing among the coal, and Four was in one of Mrs Plum's big shoes, biting the laces. Mrs Plum gathered them up, coal dust and all, and took them into the garden.

'I'll leave the other two for you to deal with,' said Mrs Plum to Minnie, settling herself under the apple tree to knit and watch the kittens.

In the kitchen, Minnie was comforting and scolding and washing at the same time. 'You're all right now and you haven't quite lost one of your nine lives,' lick – lick – lick. 'But it was very naughty of you to go upstairs alone,' lick – lick – lick. 'Now, Two, let me have another go at that tangle under your chin,' lick – lick – lick.

Mrs Plum gave them a special tea as they had all had such a tiring afternoon. There was milk, which no one spilt, and a sardine each.

'Sardines are good for you,' said Minnie, 'though there's no need to gobble. They make your fur shine.'

The Key of the Cave

Two little sisters, Rose and Mary, lived in a cottage on a rocky shore. They had never seen a train or a big town or a toyshop full of toys, but they played happily with what they had. There were, in a drawer, some beautifully dressed dolls which had been in the family for many years and were only brought out on Sundays and birthdays. There were carved wooden figures of ugly little people with long noses and pointed chins which were also precious and seldom brought down from a high shelf.

But their mother had made them knitted dolls stuffed with sheep's wool and these shabby objects were dearer than all the others. The girls took them to bed and seldom moved without them.

Though Rose and Mary could play anywhere in the bay where the cottage was built, they were not allowed to go round the jutting rocks into the next bay without their father or mother. But there was plenty of room in their own bay and they knew every rock. They gave them names, Seaweed Rock, Limpet Rock, Shell Rock, and Elephant Rock. They made houses for their dolls under the rocks, and gardens on top of them, planted with tufts of seaweed.

'We are getting older now,' said Rose one day, at breakfast.

'I can tie my boots and do up my back buttons,' said Mary.

'We are old enough to go round the point into the next bay,' said Rose. 'No harm could come to us.'

'Why do you want to go there specially?' asked their mother. 'There is more sand here, on our own beach.'

'But there are better shells,' said the girls. 'We can find razor shells and scallops as big as saucers and many others. Please let us go.'

Their father and mother looked at each other and their father shook his head.

'No,' he said firmly, 'not by yourselves.'

'Is it because of the Echoing Cave?' asked Rose.

'Yes. The Echoing Cave is no place for children. It is no place for anybody. The twisting passages leading from it into the cliff-side are so dangerous that many a soul has gone a few yards to explore, and has never seen the light of day again.'

Rose and Mary had been as far as the mouth of this cave many times with their parents. The cave gave back a very clear echo and it amused them to shout and whistle and call, and hear the sound that came rolling back, hollow and strange.

'May we go to the next bay if we keep out of the cave?' begged Mary, and her father, not very willingly, agreed to this.

When the spring came, Rose and Mary were even more alone than usual. Their father was out fishing and their mother had hurt her knee and was unable to walk comfortably on the uneven shore. As the weather was bright and sunny, the girls were out all day. They often went into the next bay to gather shells and it was not long before they began to think, then talk, about the Echoing Cave.

'Let's go and peep in,' suggested Rose.

'And shout just once for an echo,' added Mary.

'Then come straight out again.'

'Nothing could possibly happen to us in one little minute.'

They hurried round the point into the next bay and soon stood, hand in hand, at the mouth of the cave. The rocks were black and slippery and there was a queer smell, partly seaweed and partly stale air.

'Where are you?' shouted Rose.

'Where are you?' boomed the echo.

'Can you see me?' shouted Mary.

'Can you see me?' boomed the echo.

'Good-bye!' they both called together.

'Good-bye!' answered the echo.

They went back to play on their own beach but they kept thinking and talking of the cave, longing to go again. Soon they were visiting it every day, then twice a day, then many times, until they were spending most of their time in its gloomy shadow.

Now the girls no longer stood at the entrance, holding hands, but went boldly inside and crawled down the rocky passages that opened out in the most unexpected places, some so narrow that they could only squeeze in sideways, some so low that they had to go on hands and knees, and others hidden behind a wet curtain of seaweed.

'What are these trailing marks on the floor of the cave?' asked Mary, one day.

'They look like footprints of someone who drags his feet,' said Rose, 'but of course they couldn't be.'

'Of course not. No one ever comes here except us.'

'And they are far too long and narrow for our feet. Look! Each is as long as three of mine.'

They soon covered the sandy floor with their own prints and the other, strange ones were scuffed out of sight.

One day, their father took their mother by boat to a big

village some distance away where there was a doctor who could look at her knee. Rose and Mary were left alone, with their dinner prepared and a fruit cake for their tea.

They soon rushed through the household tasks they were left to do, and went out to play. The day was particularly sunny and warm, but their feet seemed to lead them out of the sunshine into the dark, damp shadow of the Echoing Cave.

They shouted their names and the days of the week and counted to twenty, and the echo rang back each time. But when Mary called: 'Where are you?' she looked puzzled, and so did Rose.

'Did you hear what I heard?' she asked. 'I thought the echo said "I want you".'

'So did I. Try once again.'

So Mary called again: 'Where are you?' and again the echo answered: 'I want you.'

'Where are you? Where are you?' rang out their two voices. Once more the echo came, clear and unmistakable: 'I want you.'

'We must go home at once and bolt the door and stay there,' said Rose, who knew all the while that she was disobeying her parents. 'Come along, Mary.' She took Mary's hand and began to drag her towards the mouth of the cave.

But Mary dug her heels into the sand and would not come. Her eyes shone and her cheeks were red with excitement.

'Who are you?' she called.

'I am Echo,' came back.

'Why do you want me?'

'I have something to give you.'

'Come away!' pleaded Rose, pulling at Mary's dress,

but Mary held on to a rock and would not be pulled loose.

'What is it?' she shouted.

'Something pretty,' came back the reply.

Then they noticed a green light shining from one of the rocky passages and Mary went towards it. She stopped at the entrance and held out her hand.

'Come nearer,' said the echo.

She moved forward a step.

'Nearer still.'

She took another step.

'Nearer still.'

This time she was right inside the passage, standing in the green light. There was a rumbling sound and the walls of rock moved together, like the closing of a door. The opening to the passage had disappeared. There was just a solid rocky wall, dripping with seaweed, and no sign of a crack. There was neither hinge nor handle. Mary had vanished completely.

Rose clutched at the rock, trying to find something to pull on, but there was nothing to grasp except slippery seaweed and this came off in her hands in tufts. She called her sister's name and each time she said 'Mary' the echo answered 'Mary' as if making fun of her. 'Be quiet!' she shouted at last, but only 'Be quiet!' came back to her.

As she clutched at the seaweed, clinging and tearing, Rose's fingers touched something smooth on the rough face of the rock. She tore off the surrounding seaweed and cleared a bare patch. Shining against the dark rock was a keyhole shaped like a fish's tail, outlined in mother-of-pearl. If only she had the key. Then she could unlock the door and set Mary free. But where could it be? There were hundreds of hiding-places in the cave itself and hundreds more on the cliffs and the shore. It could be anywhere.

Rose went out into the sunshine and sat on a rock and burst into tears. Almost at once a harsh, though friendly, voice near by said: 'Don't cry, Rose. There's enough salt water in the sea without you adding your tears.'

She turned her head and saw a sea gull perched beside her.

'I've plenty to cry about,' she said, the tears flowing faster than ever.

'I know,' said the sea gull. 'I was there in the cave. I saw what happened. I even screamed a warning, but you didn't understand. Now there's no time to be lost. If you want to have your sister home before your father and mother come back, you must set to work this very minute.'

'What must I do?' asked Rose, drying her eyes.

'Find the key, of course.'

'But it might be anywhere.'

'No,' corrected the sea gull. 'Not anywhere. Echo has one key always with him, but he keeps a spare one hidden. I've heard that a crab is taking care of it for him.'

'Then we must find a crab. Where shall we look for one?' asked Rose. 'And what shall we do when we've found one?'

'You must rap three times on its shell like this,' said the sea gull, giving three sharp taps on a stone with his beak. 'Then you must say:

> Crab, Crab,
> Have you the key?
> Crab, Crab,
> Please give it to me.

'We'll search the cave first.'

There were a few small pools near the walls of the cave, left by a high tide. Rose began looking in these, lifting mats of seaweed, and putting her hand under shelves of rock. Presently she saw a crab scuttling across the sandy floor. She made a dive for him.

'Hold him with your finger and thumb at each end,' said the sea gull. 'Then he can't nip you.'

Rose gripped him in the way recommended, and lifted him up. He was a green crab. She tapped on his shell with her other hand and said:

> Green crab, green crab,
> Have you the key?
> Green crab, green crab,
> Please give it to me.

The crab growled, waving his claws in the air:

> I have no key
> And that is true,
> I have no key
> To give to you.

Rose set him down in the pool and he went off sideways.

Then she saw a movement under some brown seaweed and put out her hand and grasped a crab with blue claws. She tapped three times on his shell:

> Crab with blue claws,
> Have you the key?
> Crab with blue claws,
> Please give it to me.

The crab was silent for a minute and then said sadly:

> I have no key
> And that is true,
> I have no key
> To give to you.

The next crab was found by the sea gull. He had tufts of seaweed growing on his shell and he looked like a seaweed-covered stone. Rose could not find a bare place on his shell to tap, so she tapped on his claw instead.

> Tufted crab, tufted crab,
> Have you the key?
> Tufted crab, tufted crab,
> Please give it to me.

She felt sure the key was hidden among the tufts and she was disappointed when the crab said:

> I have no key
> And that is true,
> I have no key
> To give to you.

As the day wore on they found other crabs, some big enough to be frightening, and some little spider crabs with thin legs and small round bodies. None of them was any help.

All the morning they worked, Rose never even thinking of the dinner waiting for her on the table, and the sea gull never stopping to catch a fish for himself.

By the middle of the afternoon Rose was stiff with bending down and it was painful to straighten her back for a rest. Her head ached and she felt sick from the hot sun on the back of her neck. The sea gull was in a worse plight than she, because flying was his usual way of getting about, and walking was both awkward and tiring. The sun was lower in the sky and dazzled their eyes as they searched. Rose knew the boat with her parents on board would soon be back.

There was a whelk shell lying on the beach. Rose picked

it up and put it to her ear because whelk shells have the sound of the sea inside them. But this one was quiet. No murmur of the waves could be heard. Instead, a thin little voice cried:

'This is my home. I'm a hermit crab.'

Rose took the shell from her ear at once and looked inside. She could see the crab's face and one claw which was poking out.

'Is it nice in there?' she asked.

'It was nice once,' said the hermit crab. 'Very nice indeed. Safe and comfortable. But there's something strange inside with me and there isn't room for both.'

'What is it like?' asked Rose.

'I don't really know. But it's long and pointed and sharp at one end. A useless sort of thing. I wish I could get rid of it.'

The sea gull and Rose looked at each other. Could it be, might it be, what they were searching for?

'If I find you another empty shell to live in, would you like to move?' said Rose.

'Indeed I would. But you must watch while I run from one shell to the other. I have no hard back like most crabs. Any person who is hungry' – he looked at the sea gull – 'could gobble me up in a moment.'

Rose found a perfect empty shell and told the sea gull to keep out of sight. Then the hermit crab, who was a poor, soft, tender person, ran safely from one to the other. He curled up in his new home, sighing to himself:

'How comfortable! How safe! Nothing sharp digging into me. Just myself in my own house.'

Then, quick as a flash, Rose picked up his old home and shook it. Something inside rattled. She shook again and out fell a beautiful little key made of yellow amber, shaped like a fish's tail.

Rose ran back to the cave, the sea gull flying in circles round her head, and she fumbled in the bare patch for the keyhole. For a moment she thought that it, too, had disappeared, but then she saw its pearly gleam. The key slid easily into the lock and as she turned it, the rocky door swung open. In the dim green light she saw the scarlet of Mary's jersey and seized hold of it and pulled. At first she felt someone pulling against her, pulling Mary backwards, but Mary herself was straining with all her might towards the door. When they were both safely over the threshold and in the cave, the door closed behind them.

They heard a deep voice calling: 'Mary! Mary! Come back!' Then there was silence.

'Oh Mary, how I've missed you.'

'Oh Rose, you don't know how frightened I was.'

They held hands and smiled at each other.

'Hurry off home,' prompted the sea gull. 'I see the boat rounding the corner. You'll just be in time to get there first.'

They ran as fast as they could to their own bay and were in time to welcome their mother and to help their father to tie up the boat. Their mother was already walking better as the doctor had bandaged her knee firmly and comfortably.

The children's parents knew that something was wrong when they saw the untouched dinner and the uncut cake.

'Tell us exactly what has happened,' they said, and Rose and Mary told them everything, though Mary had little to say about the hours she had spent walled in the rocky cave.

'It was dark,' she said, again and again. 'It was dark with a dim green light, and I was frightened and I cried. When I cried Echo cried too. He was gentle but so strange. He stroked my arm and I shivered because he was so clammy.'

'What was the pretty thing?' asked Rose suddenly. 'I've only just remembered about it.'

'I'd forgotten too,' said Mary, 'but here it is.' She stretched out her hand and on one finger was a ring set with a pearl. 'He said I could have a ring for every finger if I'd stay with him for always.'

'We'll give the sea gull a good breakfast tomorrow,' said their mother. 'It was really he who rescued you. Now go to bed and be thankful we are all safe under our own roof.'

The Wandering Snow-man

It seemed to the children as if the snow had come to stay for ever. Each morning when they woke up, there were frosty pictures of ferns and mountains on the window and when they rubbed a patch of ice away and looked out, the garden was still white.

They could hardly sit down and eat their breakfast, they wanted so badly to be outside, playing. At last, warm inside from their hot porridge, coats buttoned up, hoods tied under chins, Wellingtons pulled over thick socks, they were allowed to run outside.

The garden was quiet and strange at first. A little more snow had fallen while they were asleep and covered up the marks of their feet and the tracks of the sledge, left from yesterday. But the two boys, Billy and Tim, soon began to throw snow-balls at each other, and they laughed and shouted, stumbled and tumbled, till the garden did not feel strange any more.

Their two little sisters, Rose and Jean, were not fond of snow-balling. They took their sea-side pails and made snow-pies with them, instead of sand-pies. They decorated their snow-pies with leaves and berries and tasted them with the tips of their tongues.

'Mine is a strawberry ice-cream,' said Rose.

'Mine is an iced lolly,' said Jean.

The day before, the children had all made snow-men. Billy and Tim made a big snow-man and the little girls made what they called a 'snow-child'. The snow child was small and thin and looked unhappy. The boys' big snow-man was large and fat and seemed a jolly fellow. Today the boys had a new idea.

'We'll make a house,' they shouted. 'An igloo like an Eskimo house. Come on, get two spades and we'll begin. It will be hard work, building a real igloo.'

Billy had seen a picture of an igloo in a book.

'Mark out a circle,' he said, and Tim marked out a big circle.

'Now we must cut blocks of snow with our spades and put them round the circle. Then we pile another layer on top, overlapping a bit. Then another layer, and another and another.'

It was hard work indeed. Their faces were as red as their scarves and their arms ached, but they did not stop for a rest. Shovelling – placing – trimming – smoothing – there was not a moment to spare. The igloo began to take shape like a big white beehive.

Rose and Jean had gone indoors long ago to have their cold hands blown on and rubbed by their mother and their socks and scarves hung on the fire-guard to dry. Then, warm and comfortable once more, they sat on the rug to have a dolls' tea-party. Once they looked through the window and saw the boys still working hard and the igloo nearly finished.

There was one round hole in the middle of the roof to fill up. The boys scooped out a door and Billy crept inside and reached up and filled the hole. The igloo was complete except for a few last touches. The boys took handfuls of loose snow and filled the cracks between the layers, patting it down.

'Someone could really live in it,' said Tim. 'Someone like an Eskimo or a polar bear.'

'Or a snow-man,' said Billy and laughed. They crawled out of the door on hands and knees just as their mother called them in for dinner.

The children were hungry and Billy and Tim had three helpings of jam roly-poly. Then, feeling tired, they had their rest and settled down to go through their stamp albums. They knew every stamp in their own and each other's album but they were never tired of looking at them and counting them.

After tea, there was a mew at the back door and in dashed their kitten, Flick. Flick's hair was standing on end and his eyes were round with surprise. He dived under the sofa and hid there.

'What has frightened poor Flick?' asked the children. 'There's no dog in the garden.'

'He just feels small in a big, white world,' said mother, pouring some milk into his saucer.

'I think he has seen something,' said Billy. 'Mother, do please let Tim and me go out for a few minutes? It's not dark and we want to make sure our igloo is safe.'

'Please say "yes",' added Tim. 'We won't make a single snow-ball or get wet. And we won't get snow in our Wellingtons, either.'

'Very well,' said their mother. 'But do be careful. I've dried enough wet things for today.'

The boys scrambled into their coats and boots and hurried into the garden. The igloo looked even better in the twilight. As they drew nearer, they stopped short and stood without moving. There were voices murmuring inside the igloo.

'It was a good idea to build us a house,' said someone gruffly.

'If they did build it for us,' said another. 'I heard them mention Eskimoes and polar bears.'

'*And* snow-men,' said the first voice. 'They said "snow-men" plainly.'

'It's really very snug inside. I'm glad we made this snow couch to sit on. My legs were beginning to ache, standing out there in the garden day and night.'

'Yes, it's snug enough. But you are lucky. You have a warm hat and a pipe to smoke. Those horrid children next door did not give me anything like that. Why, I've only one eye.'

'I'd like a pipe,' said a squeaky voice.

'Don't be silly. You're only a snow-baby. Snow-babies can't smoke pipes. And you have four nice buttons.'

'But I do want a pipe,' went on the squeaky voice. 'I want a pipe of my very own.'

'Be quiet!' scolded the gruff voice. 'Tomorrow, if you're good. I'll give you a lovely cold icicle to suck. I know where there is a beauty.'

Billy and Tim crept as close as they dared and crouched down and peered through the low door, but it was too dark inside to see anything plainly. Then their mother called and they had to creep away towards the house.

'You're very quiet,' said their mother. 'Are you all right?'

'Oh yes. Quite all right. But a bit tired. May we have our baths before the girls for once? They didn't do hard work like us.'

A little later, they were both in a deep, hot bath.

'Did you hear what I heard?' asked Billy through the steam.

'I suppose so. The gruff one was our snow-man, I'm sure.'

'I'm glad we gave him a pipe and daddy's old hat.'

'So am I. Poor old next-door one. We must see what we can do for him tomorrow. I wonder how many were in the igloo?'

'I don't know. I only heard three voices.'

'So did I.'

The next morning the windows were once again frosted over when Billy and Tim jumped out of bed. They began breathing on the glass and rubbing with their fingers. They could see the igloo shining in the morning sun as though it had been dusted all over with powdered glass. The snow-man was once more standing on the lawn, hat on head and pipe in mouth, and the snow-child was in her place near the holly bush. They could see the one-eyed snow-man next door.

'I suppose – I suppose what we heard last night was true,' said Tim doubtfully.

'It must have been as we both heard it. We shall know it is true if we find a snow couch in the igloo.'

Breakfast was over at last and the children rushed out into the clear blue morning. The boys crawled into the igloo and were pleased to see a low ridge of snow which they had certainly not made themselves. It was the snow couch.

Rose and Jean were patting their snow-child into shape. 'Look!' they cried. 'She has an icicle in her mouth. She likes sucking icicles just as we do.'

The next-door children came out to play and the boys persuaded them to give their snow-man a second eye and some buttons. The girls gave their snow-child a necklace of holly berries and a crown of holly leaves, to make her pretty.

Billy and Tim spent the rest of the morning making a dog for the snow-man. The dog was very difficult indeed. His legs would not bear him and collapsed one after the other. His tail fell off and his ears melted under their warm fingers. They decided to make a sitting-down dog instead and this was much easier. With a shoe lace round his neck for a collar, he was as good a dog as you could wish to see. He sat at the snow-man's feet in a protecting way.

After tea, the boys were longing to visit the igloo as before. Billy had his father's bicycle lamp ready as they wanted to see for themselves what was happening inside.

'May we go and see the sunset?' they asked.

'And make sure the igloo is safe for the night?'

'We'll keep dry as snuff, as we did last time.'

'Very well,' said their mother and they tugged on their coats and boots. They tip-toed over the lawn, wishing the frosty snow did not crackle, and stopped near the igloo. They could hear voices inside.

'I shall call him Spark,' said the gruff voice.

'Bow-wow! Bow-wow!' barked a dog.

'Good. He likes his name. What a lucky day this has been for us all. Spark will be a real friend to me. I shall never be lonely with him near by.'

'And I've been given this pretty crown and necklace,' squeaked the snow-child.

'And I've a new eye — in the right place, too — and a stylish row of buttons. What about you, Mr Top Hat?'

'I've had a very tiring day,' replied Mr Top Hat. 'The children at the end house pelted me with snow-balls, trying to knock my hat off. When they were successful, they shrieked and shouted with joy and put my hat back and started all over again.'

'Anyhow, it's a very fine hat,' said another voice. 'Very fine. Fit for a wedding. I believe you said the lining was real silk.'

'Yes, real silk,' agreed Mr Top Hat proudly.

'I'm going to switch on the lamp,' whispered Billy and a bright beam lit up the inside of the igloo. They saw about half a dozen white figures, sitting on the couch, with snow-dog on the floor and snow-child playing with something in a corner. They recognized several of the figures as snow-men they had seen in other gardens, up and down the road. All conversation stopped as the light flashed and no one moved.

'Please don't mind us,' said Billy politely. 'We just wanted to see if you were comfortable in here. You'll be all right till the morning as the thaw hasn't begun yet. The ice is still thick on the puddles. Good night.'

'Good night,' added Tim. The snow-men appeared to bow slightly but they did not speak. Billy switched off the lamp and they went away. They thought they heard Spark barking as they closed the back door.

The next day was just as crisp and clear and cold and the children played with their sledges. What would happen when the thaw set in? They did not like to imagine. The air felt milder already as they went indoors for tea.

In the middle of the night Billy whispered to Tim:

'Can you hear water dripping?'

'Yes. It's the icicles melting.'

'I heard a sliding noise as if snow were sliding off the roof.'

'The thaw has begun. Whatever will they do in the igloo?'

'I don't know. Isn't it awful?'

'We must get up early and warn them about the thaw.'

'But what can we do to help?'

'We can't really do anything.'

They dressed earlier than usual and saw that there was no frost on their window. They unlocked the back door and went out. The snow was softer than before and wetter. Billy went up to their big snow-man.

'It's thawing,' he said.

'I know,' replied the snow-man. 'It was quite hot last night in the igloo. My nose began to drip.'

'So did mine,' put in the snow-child, 'and my feet tingled. I hardly slept a wink.'

'Nor did Spark,' said his master. 'He was fidgeting and panting all night.'

'What are you going to do?' asked Tim anxiously.

'Melt,' said the snow-man.

'What about the snow-child? She's so young.'

'She'll melt as well. In fact she'll melt quicker as she's smaller. I doubt whether she'll last a couple of days. Now I am a man of substance. I reckon I shall last the best part of a week. Long life runs in the family.'

'Don't you mind?' asked Billy.

'Mind what?'

'Mind melting, of course.'

'No, why should I? I'm tired of being on the ground. I shall be a cloud next and that will be a nice change. Just floating along – floating along – high in the sky.'

'Shall I be a cloud too?' asked the snow-child.

'Why not? All snow people turn into clouds. We melt. We turn to water. The sun dries us up and changes us into clouds. Later on, we may come back to the earth as snow-flakes.'

The thaw was a slow one. It was nearly a week before the grass of the lawn showed green and eight days before the little heaps of snow that were once Spark and the snow-child had completely disappeared. The snow-man stood firm. He lost his shape and his eyes and nose and mouth had gone long ago, but he was still a good, solid pillar of white.

The boys visited him every morning to cheer him up.

The white pillar grew shorter and thinner and after three weeks it was gone.

'How we shall miss him!' sighed Billy.

'He said he'd come back next year as snowflakes and we could make him into a man again.'

'I know. But there are such millions and millions of snowflakes. We shall never know which are especially his.'

The holidays ended and school began again, so the boys had not so much time to play in the garden and wonder about the snowman.

One lovely sunny morning, they were running home when Tim said, 'Look! Look at those white clouds. What do they remind you of?'

Billy stared upwards and saw a tall, white, solid-looking cloud hurrying across the sky with a little one at his heels, and just behind, a small fluffy figure with outstretched arms.

'It's the snow-man,' he gasped, 'with Spark at his heels and the little snow-child trying to catch up.'

Sea Baby

ONE cold wintry day a fisherman was fishing. It was getting late. The sun was setting and it would soon be dark. He had fished all day but had caught nothing. He decided to cast his net once more before he went home. He cast it out into the grey water.

When he pulled the net in, it felt heavy. He knew that he had caught something. Perhaps it was a fine cod or a flounder. He looked forward to a good supper that night.

As he drew the net out of the water, there was no silvery gleam of fish's scales. There was only a little naked boy, as bare as a sea shell. The child was curled up in a ball, with his arms hugging his chest, and his knees drawn up.

'Here's a pretty kettle of fish,' said the man. 'I never expected to catch a baby. Don't be afraid, little one. No one will harm you.'

He lifted the little boy out of the net and tried to wrap him in his own scarf. But when the child felt hands on him he turned and twisted like an eel. It was all the fisherman could do to wind the scarf round the small, struggling body. Then he carried the child carefully home, holding tightly to the woollen bundle.

It was dark when the fisherman got home and opened the door of his hut.

'Have you had any luck?' asked his wife.

'I'm not sure if it's good luck or bad luck,' he said.

'Well, have you caught any fish?'

'No, not any fish, but I caught something. Look here.' He unrolled the scarf and set the child on the hearth rug.

'Oh, the darling!' said his wife. 'The little treasure! Come to me and let me warm you,' and she held out her arms.

But the child darted away and hid in the darkest corner of the hut, under the bed.

The fisherman coaxed, and his wife coaxed, and they lay on the floor and pleaded with him to come out. At last they moved the bed and the fisherman caught him and held him.

'Keep him safe,' said his wife, 'and I'll see if there is anything in the hut for him to wear. He'll catch his death of cold as he is.'

Their own children were grown up and out in the world, but she managed to find a blue jersey and a pair of blue trousers. But though the fisherman held him fast, the two of them could not get clothes on him. He would not have the jersey over his head, or his arms in the sleeves. Neither would he put his legs into the trousers.

'Well,' said the fisherman at last. 'Let him be without clothes if he has a mind to be like that. After all, he wore not a stitch when I drew him out of the sea in my net. And it was colder than our hut, under the dark waves. Let him be.'

So they let him be, and he crept away under the bed.

'We must feed him,' said the wife. 'A baby needs good food. I'll make him some porridge.'

She made a bowl of porridge and put sugar on it, and the top of the milk, just the way children relish it. Then she tried to feed the sea baby with a spoon, while her husband held him.

But not a bite nor a sup would the sea baby have. When

it was forced between his lips, he spat it out. At last, worn out, they had their own supper and went to bed. The sea baby curled up in a corner and lay still. As they lay awake, they could hear his soft breathing.

More than once, the fisherman or his wife got out of bed and tried to take him in their arms and nurse him, but he slipped through their hands like a slippery fish.

Two days passed and the sea baby would neither wear clothes nor eat food. The fisherman began to think he should put the child back into the sea from whence he had been taken, but neither he nor his wife could bear to part with the little thing. He looked at them with such sad, green eyes. Once he laughed when they gave him a whelk shell to hold, and he put it to his ear. Such shells hold the sound of the sea.

'We will ask the Wise Woman what to do,' said the fisherman. 'If she cannot tell us, I'll take him back to the sea tomorrow. Maybe it is his real home.'

The Wise Woman lived in a cave a long way from the hut. The fisherman found her looking into a crystal ball, like a bubble of glass. She listened to what he had to say, never lifting her eyes from the glass ball.

'You must feed him on fish, and only on fish,' she said. 'And make him a shirt of seaweed. And give him toys from the sea shore. Then he will settle and be happy.'

The fisherman strode home as quickly as he could, and told his wife all the Wise Woman had said. 'We must feed him on fish, and dress him in a seaweed shirt, and give him toys from the sea shore.'

'Then go quickly and catch some fish. Go now!' said his wife.

Luckily he soon caught a fine fish. While his wife was

making fish soup and little fish cakes, he went back to the beach and gathered an armful of seaweed.

Soon the sea baby was supping his soup, and eating the fish cakes, and soon the wife had sewn strips of brown and green seaweed into a shirt. She put this on him and he stood still, and laughed to see himself in the mirror.

As the days passed, the fisherman found him toys from the sea shore. There were striped pebbles, and shiny ones; bits of bare stick with the bark eaten off by the sea, and shells of many kinds. The sea baby played with these for hours.

Once the fisherman brought him a stone with a hole in it, and the sea baby threw his arms round his neck and kissed him.

The sea baby grew up to be a fine fisherman and a great swimmer and a good son to his new father and mother. Never had parents a dearer son. Never had son more loving parents.

Go to Sleep, Shellover

WHILE Shellover was telling the last story, *Sea Baby*, he grew sleepier and sleepier. Sometimes his head nodded, and his eyes closed, and his voice dropped to a whisper.

'Stay awake a little longer,' barked the Dog. 'Just finish this one story.'

'Yes, just finish this one story,' mewed the Cat.

'Just this one story,' mooed the Cow.

'Just this one story,' clucked the Hens.

Mrs Candy said nothing, but stroked his head gently.

Then Shellover gave his head a jerk. Opened his eyes. His voice grew stronger. But as he said the last few words, 'Never had son more loving parents', he fell fast asleep.

The pets looked uneasy. Had they done wrong in urging him on to finish? Had they been unkind to their friend? But Mrs Candy comforted them.

'We'll bury him ourselves, tomorrow,' she said. 'We know the exact spot, and just how he likes to be settled in. You can all help.'

So the next morning Shellover was buried, very gently and carefully, under the laurel bush.

'Good night, Shellover,' said all his friends. 'Sleep well!'

At first they missed Shellover's stories badly. Often one of them would retell an old story to the others. But they got so they knew them all by heart.

The evenings were long and dark, and they missed Shell-over's cheerful voice. Then, one day, Mrs Candy said:

'Shall we try to make up some stories for ourselves? We can't expect to tell such wonderful stories as Shellover – he is a born story-teller – but it might help to pass the time. Who would like to begin?'

The Cat said she would try first, so she jumped on to Mrs Candy's lap and began:

'I'll tell you how I lost one of my nine lives, the very first of them,' she said. 'This happened long ago, when I was a kitten. My mother only allowed us to play on the grass near the house, because she knew we would be safe there. But I was a naughty little kitten and I wanted to explore the rest of the garden for myself. So when she was busy bathing my brother and sister, I slipped out and ran away.

'When I got to the vegetable garden I met a smart, large animal in a sandy coat.

' "You are very young to be out alone," said the smart animal.

' "It is the first time," I said, "and my mother doesn't know I am out."

' "Come to my den and have supper with me and my family," said Sandy Coat.

' "I only like milk and fish-without-bones," I said.

' "Why, that's just what we are having for supper tonight" said Sandy Coat. "I'm sure you will enjoy it."

'We went through hedges, and over fields, and across a bridge, till we got to a cave in the rocks where Sandy Coat lived.

'But there was no milk, and no fish-without-bones. There was an untidy, dirty den that smelt musty and fusty, and there was Sandy Coat's wife with a hungry look on her face, and Sandy Coat's three children with a hungry look on their faces.

' "What have you brought for supper?" asked his wife.

' "What have you brought for supper?" asked his children.

' "This," said Sandy Coat, holding me by the scruff of my neck.

' "Better than nothing," said Sandy Coat's wife, "but hardly enough for us all. You go and find something else more suitable for a family of foxes. I'll prepare this creature for the pot while you are away."

'So I was in a fox's den. I shivered and shook with fear and my teeth chattered. How I wished I were back at home.

' "What kind of thing are you?" asked Mrs Fox.

' "I'm a kitten," I said in a trembling voice.

' "Do you know how you ought to be cooked? I've never cooked a kitten before."

' "Oh yes," I replied. "First you must find some sprigs of peppercorn to give me flavour, and to make me tender."

' "What does peppercorn look like?" said Mrs Fox.

' "Oh, its very common," I said. "It's leaves are grey and it has black seeds on it, like little black bells. I'll find some in a jiffy."

' "Be quick about it," said Mrs Fox. "My cubs will help you."

'So I went off with the three cubs, but I soon set them to search in different places. At first I pretended to search near the den, where Mrs Fox could watch me, but I gradually got further and further away. The moment I was out of sight of the den, I ran for my life, and never stopped running till I was in my mother's furry arms.

'She washed me all over to get rid of the foxy smell, and

then I had bread-and-milk for supper. That is how I lost the first of my nine lives.'

The other pets all said how glad they were that the Cat had not been eaten by the family of foxes. Mrs Candy tickled him under his chin, and said thank you for the story.

The seven Hens had been clucking and clacking and putting their heads together in a corner. Now they stood in a row and said:

'We are going to recite a poem.'

'It has seven lines.'

'We are going to say one line each.'

The Hen at one end said the first line, and the others followed in turn:

> Seven black hens lay snow white eggs,
> Seven black hens have yellow legs,
> Seven black hens like corn to eat,
> Seven black hens like greens for a treat,
> Seven black hens perch in a row,
> Seven black hens to the farmyard go,
> Seven black hens are Mrs Candy's friend,
> Now our poem has come to an end.

Everyone clapped and cheered, and asked to have the poem again. So the hens lined up and said it through a second time.

'I never knew I had seven poets in my hen-run,' said Mrs Candy, stroking their smooth black feathers.

Then came the Cow's turn. She was rather worried, and kept moving her head from side to side uneasily. Mrs Candy knew just how she was feeling, and she went to the window to stroke the Cow's soft cheek.

'Please yourself, dear Cow,' she said. 'You can tell a story

another time, or not at all if it worries you. We all understand.'

'I do know a story,' said the Cow, 'but I'm afraid you
won't believe me, though it is a true story.'

'We will believe every word,' said the pets. 'Really
we will.' So the Cow, hanging her head with shyness,
began:

'One day I was strolling round my buttercup meadow in
the sun and I thought I would have a short nap. So I lay
down and closed my eyes. When I woke up, I found I could
not move from the place where I lay. Somehow I was a
prisoner. I looked up, and saw that I was surrounded by
hundreds of tiny people dressed in green. They were about
as tall as Mrs Candy's little finger. They must have been
working very hard while I slept, as they had plaited hundreds of grassy ropes, and these were attached to each hoof
and to my tail and to my horns. Of course I could have
broken one rope easily, but hundreds of them were strong
enough, together, to keep me securely tied.

' "Why have you done this?" I asked. "I have never
harmed you."

' "We know that," said their leader, who wore a gold
chain round his neck. "But we want you to do something
for us, and it is so important that we could not risk you
saying no. That's why we made you a prisoner."

' "What is this important thing?" I asked.

' "Come with us for an hour and do what we want, and
then you can come back to this very spot. No harm shall
come to you."

'I never doubted that he spoke the truth, so I said:

' "Let me free from these ropes, and I will follow you."

'Quickly they unloosened the hundreds of grass ropes that

121

held me, and I got to my feet and went with them. Their leader sat on my head, between my horns, and gave me directions, whispering in my ear.

'We crossed several fields till we came to a green, grassy hill. A door in the hillside opened, and out came more little people, dressed in green. Among them was a lady with a crown on her head. Everyone bowed low to her, and I bowed with them. She was the Queen of the fairies.

'She held in her arms a little baby who was crying bitterly.

' " My baby son is very ill," said the Queen, "and the

Wise Woman tells me that only a bath in cow's milk will cure him. Will you give me some of your milk?"

'I agreed, and twenty little milk-maids came up to me with milking pails in their hands. But they were too small to milk me.

' "Bring tall ladders," called the leader with the gold chain, and these proved just long enough for the milk-maids to do their milking. Their tiny hands were light as thistle-down, but it was their milking song that seemed to charm the milk from me. Soon the pails were full.

'The milk was poured into a bath and the baby prince was put in it. At once his cries stopped, and he changed into a sleepy, happy baby.

' "He is better," said the Queen, looking at him joyfully. "Now what can I give you as a reward?"

' "There's nothing I want," I said. "Mrs Candy takes care of me, and I have many friends."

' "Then I will put a royal mark on you," she said, "to show that I and all my people are grateful to you. Lower your head a little."

'I lowered my head so that she could touch the tip of each horn with her finger. That is why I have a speck of gold on the tips of my horn to this very day.'

The pets asked dozens of questions about fairies, and were allowed to touch the gold tips for themselves.

'Now I'll tell you my story,' barked the Dog impatiently, and he began in a deep, important voice:

'Once upon a time there was a Dog, who lived at peace with the world, and only barked when a stranger came in the gate. He was digging in the garden for a bone he had buried some days before, when he dug up not his old bone, but a new, clean, shiny wish-bone. It hadn't a shred of meat on it, but the Dog liked the look of it, just the same. He took it carefully to his kennel, and hid it at the back, in the straw.

'That night, when the Dog had been asleep a little while, he heard a tiny voice whispering:

' "Give me back my bone!"

' "I won't. It's my bone now," said the Dog, and he went to sleep again.

'Later on he heard a louder voice saying:

' "Give me back my bone!"

124

' "I won't. It's my bone now," said the Dog, and he went to sleep again.

'Later on he heard a still louder voice, loud as the wind, saying:

' "Give me back my bone!"

' "I won't. It's my bone now," said the Dog, and he went to sleep again.

'Later on he heard an even louder voice, loud as thunder, saying:

' "GIVE ME BACK MY BONE!"

' "I won't. It's my bone now," said the Dog. But instead of going back to sleep, he looked out of the door of his kennel. The moon was shining, and he saw a dog as big as a calf, with eyes that turned round and round, and whose back bristled like a hedge. As he looked, the big dog yawned and showed enormous white teeth.

' "GIVE ME BACK MY BONE!" said the giant dog, in his voice like thunder.

'The Dog did not wait to be asked again. He quickly found the bone and tossed it out of his kennel. Then the giant dog turned, and went away.

'In the morning, the Dog saw footprints in the garden as big as horse's hoofs. He never saw his wish-bone again, but he never saw the giant dog either, except, sometimes, in dreams.'

'Is that all?' said the pets.

'Yes,' said the Dog.

'Shellover told much longer stories,' grumbled the Hens, but Mrs Candy smiled, and said:

'A very nice story indeed, with a happy ending. You're a clever Dog,' and she patted him, and he wagged his tail.

'Now we must go to bed,' said Mrs Candy, and she saw that all her children were comfortably settled before she went to bed herself. Before she fell asleep, she thought of Shellover under the laurel bush slumbering peacefully.

If you have enjoyed reading this book and would like to know about others which we publish, why not join the Puffin Club? You will be sent the club magazine, *Puffin Post*, four times a year and a smart badge and membership book. You will also be able to enter all the competitions. For details of cost and an application form, send a stamped addressed envelope to:

The Puffin Club Dept A
Penguin Books Limited
Bath Road
Harmondsworth
Middlesex